MAX MAGIC

THE GREATEST SHOW ON EARTH

The Max Magic series

Max Magic

The Greatest Show on Earth

Praise for

'Max Magic is **the best book I've ever read**. It's so funny and I love learning all the magic tricks too!'

Marlow, aged 10

'I really loved Max Magic, and I got a magic set at Christmas so that I could practise tricks! **Lucky the dog is amazing** too. I can't wait to read the next book!'

Lana, aged 7

'I loved Max Magic so much that **now I want to be a magician!** I've started learning tricks. It was really cool!'

Leo, aged 8

'I loved the way Max and his friends stood up to Bottley and other bullies. Trying out the different magic tricks was great fun too. **I give it 5 stars.**'

Evie, aged 7

'Max Magic was so fun to read with my daddy, and **we** loved trying the magic tricks from the videos!'

Imogen, aged 7

'I liked it because **it had lots of magic in it, which I love!**'

Leon, aged 7

'Max Magic is fascinating and adventurous. I learn new words and I love the magic bits. Oh . . . and I love Stephen Mulhern too. **Unbelievable!**'

Millie, aged 8

MAX MAGIC

THE GREATEST SHOW ON EARTH

STEPHEN MULHERN

with TOM EASTON ♠ illustrated by
Begoña Fernández Corbalán

Piccadilly
PRESS

To Pamela, who always buys my books and makes me the best bacon sandwiches. – T.E.

First published in Great Britain in 2023 by
PICCADILLY PRESS
4th Floor, Victoria House, Bloomsbury Square, London WC1B 4DA
Owned by Bonnier Books, Sveavägen 56, Stockholm, Sweden
www.bonnierbooks.co.uk/PiccadillyPress

A CIP catalogue record for this book is available from the British Library.

ISBN: 978-1-80078-382-9
Signed edition ISBN: 978-1-80078-709-4
Also available as an ebook and in audio

1

Typeset in Easy Reading Pro

EasyReading® Font
High-legibility typeface

Interior design by Nigel Baines. Illustrations by Begoña Fernández Corbalán
Inside cover illustrated doodles © Shutterstock
Author photograph © @Oliver_Rosser // @FeastCreative
Printed and bound in Great Britain by Clays Ltd, Elcograf S.p.A.

Piccadilly Press is an imprint of Bonnier Books UK
www.bonnierbooks.co.uk

Hello,

First of all, thank you so much for taking
the time to read my new book!

In every book I write there will always be a
message to take from it. One that I hope you will
remember for a long time to come.

The thing to remember in this book is something I
was taught from a very young age, and here it is:

Even if you can't change the people around you, you
can change the people you choose to be around.

Things aren't over if you fail or make a mistake –
things are only over if you don't get back up
and make that mistake right!

All will become clear as you read
Max Magic: The Greatest Show on Earth!

Remember – whatever you do in life, never give up!

Old Dogs and New Tricks

'Wake up, Max! It's an emergency!'

I sat bolt upright, confused and disoriented but ready to face whatever danger threatened. My pet dog Lucky stared back at me from the foot of the bed, eyes wide.

'What is it, Lucky?' I asked, scanning

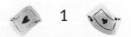

the room for the burglar, or the fire, or the huge demon from the Nether Dimensions. 'What's the emergency?'

'I'm hungry!' Lucky said.

'What? That's not an emergency! You're always hungry!'

'You don't understand, Max,' Lucky replied with a little whiny growl. 'Your mum has bought Wacky Dog instead of Waggy Boy.'

I suppose I should explain at this point, just in case this is the first time you've met me. I'm Max Magic, and one day I'll be Max the Magnificent! Well, that's my dream – and believe me, dreams **can** come true . . . My dog Lucky is a very special dog indeed. He can talk. Or at least, I can understand him, which might not be the same thing. I have to admit I don't really get how it all works, but ever since I opened a magic chest in my gran's antique shop a few weeks ago, I've been able to understand everything Lucky says. And I have to say, a lot of it is total rubbish.

I've been able to do other things too. Magical things. Extraordinary things. And, sometimes, terrifying things. Because when I opened that chest, there was a flash and a bang. I fell backwards and bumped my head, and when I woke up I discovered I had three magical powers. Telekinesis – moving things with just the power of my mind; telepathy – reading people's minds; and illusion – making objects appear, like

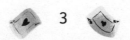

3

monsters (and, once, a giant worm).

Most of the time, being able to talk to my dog is brilliant. But sometimes he can be extremely annoying. Especially when he's hungry, which is most of the time.

'So?' I asked with a groan. I sat up in bed, stretched and yawned.

'So, they are not the same,' Lucky said. He jumped down onto the floor and ran around the room, agitated. 'Waggy Boy is 100% pure meat, carved off the bone. Wacky Dog is 100% bits of something a bit meaty scraped off the floor.'

'Wacky Dog is cheaper,' I pointed out.

'I can't believe you're on your mum's side over this,' Lucky said, shaking his head sadly.

'Hey, I have to eat Hoonz baked beans

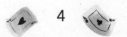

from the Lo-Cost supermarket,' I said.
'We're all in this together.'

'Were your baked beans jet-washed off
the floor of the Hoonz factory?'

I was about to answer, but then I
smelled the delicious scent of bacon frying
downstairs. I grinned. Bacon was a real
treat in our house these days. 'Come on,' I
said. 'Let's go and have breakfast.'

Downstairs, we found the usual chaos.
Dad was in the kitchen, pop music blaring.
At the same time he was shouting at Andrea,
the smart-home device he'd bought from a
dodgy stall down the market and which he'd
been having a long-running battle with.
Lately it had only been speaking in Spanish
for some reason.

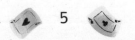 5

'Andrea, volume up!' he yelled.

'No se eso,' Andrea replied.

'Um, mas volumos!' Dad yelled. 'What is she saying? Andrea, volume UP!'

Everyone else had to speak up to be heard over Dad's frustrated shouting, which was so funny to watch. Mum was telling my sister Susie a story about one of her friends who worked at the hospital. At the same time Susie was telling Mum a story about one of her friends at the salon.

My brother Chris, who loves everything to do with mechanics, was tinkering with a battery pack from an e-bike.

My other brother, Vinny, was watching a football match on his tablet and giving everyone a running commentary about the deficiencies in West Ham's defence.

'Morning!' I yelled.

'**Morning!**' everyone yelled back.

'Morning!' Lucky yelled.

'Stop barking, Lucky!' Mum said. 'I can't hear myself think!'

'Unbelievable,' Lucky muttered. Of course I was the only one who could understand him; the rest of them just heard barking or whining or growling.

Dad handed me a bacon sandwich with lots of brown sauce, just how I like it.

'What's the occasion?' I asked, then took a massive mouthful.

'The new line of toys is doing really well,' Dad said. 'We might actually turn a profit this month!'

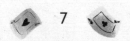

Dad ran Mullers' toy stall in Petticoat Lane Market. I helped out every day after school and also on Sundays.

'That's brilliant, Dad,' I said.

'Does this mean we can go back to buying Waggy Boy?' Lucky asked hopefully.

I winked at him and gave him a bit of my bacon.

'OW!' Chris yelled as he zapped himself with the battery pack. We all stopped chatting for a moment to check he was OK, but he ignored us and just got back to work, frowning and muttering to himself. Chris was mad about building things. But he also liked taking things apart, and he wasn't **always** able to put them back together again.

'I've got a new trick for you Max,' Dad

said. 'Maybe you can show it to Gran after dinner on Sunday.'

I grinned, though I was slightly surprised. My dad had been the first one to start me off in magic, by showing me tricks. But I sometimes got the feeling he regretted it – like when he told me that I should concentrate on schoolwork instead. These days it was mostly Gran who taught me tricks. Magic runs in the family, you could say.

Once we'd finished our bacon sarnies, Dad sat me down and pulled out a pack of cards. I had to admit I was a little disappointed. Considering I had the power to call up a wind that could destroy a marketplace, or create an illusion of a

 11

terrifying giant snake, or read the mind of any passer-by, flipping cards didn't seem like a big deal. But I watched closely while Dad ran me through the trick. First he took the cards out of the pack and showed them to me. Each card had a complicated design on the back in green and red. It looked like scales.

'Dragonscale-brand cards are the best for magicians,' he said. 'They're more expensive, but worth every penny.'

He shuffled the pack, and I watched in admiration as he flipped the cards from one hand to the other, then took half in each hand and performed what they call the blackjack shuffle. That's when you lift the corners a little, bring the two sets of cards close together and let the cards fall so the corners overlap. You then push the two halves of the pack together in a satisfying blur.

It sounds tricky and long-winded, but Dad performed it all at lightning speed. I watched in admiration. It might not have been real magic, but it sure **looked** like it.

'Pick a card, any card,' he said, fanning the cards out in front of me. I took one and looked at it. The Seven of Clubs. Dad took it from me and blew on it.

It disappeared.

I blinked in surprise. 'How did you do that?'

He winked at me. 'Magic.' He handed me the pack.

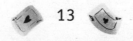

I racked my brains, trying to think how he might have done it. I guessed that when he blew on the card he quickly flipped it down into his sleeve or against his palm.

I tried three times.

The first time, as I blew on the card I tried to slip it into my sleeve, but I dropped it on the table.

The second time, as I blew on the card I accidentally spat on it.

The third time, I blew so hard on the card that it shot out of my fingers and landed in Dad's cup of tea.

'**HOW?**' I cried. 'How do you do it?!'

'You know the answer, Max,' Dad said with a grin, showing me the trick again, slowly this time. 'There's only one way to learn a new trick.'

'I know.' I sighed. 'Practice.'

'That's right,' Dad said. 'Practice. Hard work and perseverance are the most important things in life. Whether it's at school, at work, or learning a new magic trick, there are no shortcuts. I'm not sure that magic is the sort of thing that will make your fortune, or even something you can make a living at, but it teaches you discipline and patience, and that's why it's worth it.'

For a second I thought about using my powers to show him some **real** magic. With a clever illusion I could have made the card disappear. With a bit of

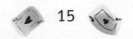 15

telekinesis I could make the card shoot across the room so fast no one could have seen it go. By doing some mind reading, I could make Dad **think** that the card had disappeared.

But that would be cheating.

Dad must have seen the look of despair on my face. He took the pack of cards back. 'Your gran used to call these her fifty-two assistants. You know, your gran once did a show where none of the props turned up – all she had was a single pack of Dragonscale cards. Even so, she held the audience spellbound for a whole hour. She made cards vanish. She did mind reading where she guessed the card people were thinking of. She threw the pack in the air blindfolded and caught the card the audience member had picked.'

I nodded. I loved hearing Dad talk about when Gran had been a real live stage magician, performing with Grandpa.

'The thing is,' he went on, 'a simple card trick can be every bit as good as a spectacular illusion.'

I nodded.

'But do you know what was the best part of that show?' he asked.

I shook my head.

'It was the patter,' he said. 'She kept up a running commentary all the way through. Little jokes. Banter. Crowd work, you know? Like . . .

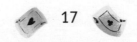

Where are you from, sir?

Bournemouth.

Sorry?

Bournemouth.

No, I heard you the first time. I'm just sorry.

'She was brilliant at that. That's what made the difference, you see. The tricks were fantastic, but more than that, she put on a proper show.' My dad learned from my gran that you can do the most unbelievable tricks in the world, but if you don't have the patter, performance and personality, nobody will ever remember. He handed me the pack again. 'I know you can talk, Max. You've got that bit sorted. But you need to work on a few more tricks. You can have this pack. Take it and learn how to use it.'

'Thanks, Dad,' I said, feeling the silky finish on the back of the Jack of Clubs. I suddenly felt determined. If Dad thought I could do it, then I wasn't going to let him down. 'Straight after school, I'm going

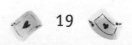 19

upstairs to my room and I'm not going to stop practising until I learn this trick.'

'Homework first,' Mum yelled from the kitchen.

Lucky groaned. 'Homework? Card tricks? I thought we were going to the park!'

Hats and Bears and Umbrellas

Lucky and I were walking to Gran's house. Gran always looked after Lucky in her shop while I was at school.

'The thing is,' I said to Lucky, 'what is the point of me spending hours on a card trick when I can read minds or make illusions?'

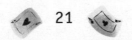

'Or you can take me to the park and throw a ball?' Lucky suggested.

'But what's the point of having magical powers when I don't even know how I should use them?' I asked. 'I know I can't use them to hurt people, or to make myself rich, or to cheat on tests. So what good are they?'

'Maybe you could magic up some more bacon?' Lucky said.

'It doesn't work like that,' I said. 'It would only be an illusion of bacon.'

'Perfect,' Lucky said. 'Tasty bacon that won't spoil your dinner.'

I laughed. 'You'd be just as hungry and start pestering me again for food straight after.'

'OK,' Lucky said. 'So how about you use your telekinesis to grab me a slice from the butcher?'

'That's stealing,' I hissed. 'Remember when I nearly took that businessman's wallet and you looked at me like I'd burned down the Houses of Parliament?'

'That's different,' he muttered, looking embarrassed. 'This is just a bit of bacon.'

We passed Happy Mike, the busker in Devonshire Square.

'Oi, Max Magic!' he cried. 'Pick a chord, any chord!'

'D minor!' I called back and he played it with a **kerrang!** I tossed a coin in the battered hat Mike had at his feet and he gave me a wink as he sang.

 23

Just then, out of the corner of my eye I saw a man come running down the street. I turned to look at him and instantly heard his thoughts, clear and strong. He was looking intently at Mike's hat.

Grab the hat! the man was thinking. I must grab the hat!

'Mike, he's going to steal your hat!' I called out.

The would-be thief bent down and made as if to seize the hat, but Mike snatched it away just in time, sending coins flying across the pavement.

The surprised thief lost his balance, tripped over his own feet and went sprawling on the pavement. He looked up to see a red-faced Mike bearing down on him, gave a yelp and sprang to his heels. The thief ran out into the road, causing a taxi to screech to a stop and honk its horn. Lucky and I trotted over to help Mike pick up his coins.

'Thanks for the warning,' Mike said, shaking his head. 'That's the third time this week someone's tried to pinch my hat. Times are tough out there – people are desperate.'

'Maybe,' I said. 'But stealing is wrong.' I gave Lucky a stern look.

'Hey, how did you know he was going to do that?' Mike said as I handed him the coins I'd collected.

I shrugged. 'Just a hunch.'

I grinned at him, and Lucky and I

 25

carried on. As we walked down Cobb Street, we saw a big dog break free of its owner's grasp and sprint down the street, barking madly. It was heading straight for Lucky, its great jaws open wide.

'Maaaaaaaax!' Lucky wailed.

I concentrated hard, and then I felt the tingle in my chest that I always got when I used my real magic.

Suddenly a massive grizzly bear appeared on the pavement between us and the dog. It looked incredibly real and incredibly angry. It thumped down on all fours, shaking the ground, and **ROARED**.

The other dog skidded to a stop, squealed in terror and raced back to its owner, tail between its legs. I chuckled.

'Erm, Max,' Lucky whispered.

I looked around to see utter chaos: dozens of people ran for their lives across the square, away from the grizzly. It was like a scene from a disaster film. The dog's owner screamed and sprinted off, overtaken by her own dog. One little boy stood a metre away from us, frozen to the spot, looking at the bear with eyes like saucers. I clicked my fingers and the illusion disappeared. The boy looked at me, as if expecting an explanation.

'Think of something – quick,' Lucky muttered.

'Er, that was a . . . hologram,' I said to the boy. 'Yes, that's right. A hologram. I think they're advertising that new bear film.

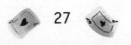

What's it called? Umm, Grizzly Graham.'

'Great work, Max,' Lucky said, rolling his eyes. 'I think we'd better get out of here.'

Just as we approached Petticoat Lane Market, a light rain began and a breeze sprang up, reminding me of the time I'd created a huge wind to defeat the Crayfish Twins. This time, though, it only caught a young woman's umbrella, tearing it from her grasp and sending it whipping up into the air. It flipped over a few times then the wind dropped and the umbrella fell, landing right in the path of a double-decker bus.

'Noooo!' the woman cried.

Almost without thinking, I stuck out my

arm and, using my telekinesis, hooked the umbrella to send it flying out of the path of the bus and back into the woman's hand. She stared at it in astonishment.

Lucky and I looked at each other. 'Nicely done,' he said.

After I'd dropped Lucky at Gran's, I headed off to school and caught up with my friends. I told them what had happened with the umbrella, the dog and the hat thief.

'That's amazing!' Daisy said. 'You should become a superhero, fighting crime. Max Magic and his Dependable Dog of Destiny!'

Sophie said, 'Maybe helping people in need is your destiny. You could use your powers to become the world's richest person and use your wealth to help the poor.'

'I think you should use your powers to become a brilliant athlete and win loads of gold medals at the Olympics,' Stretch said.

'All good ideas,' I said as we walked through the school gates. As ever, I had one eye out for the school bully, Bottley, but lately he'd been keeping a low profile. 'But these are what **you** three would do if you were magical. Daisy would be a superhero, Sophie would be a millionaire, Stretch would be a brilliant gymnast. But you will already achieve those amazing

things even **without** magic. I've got all
these powers and I don't even know what to
do with them. I mean, come on – returning
umbrellas? Guarding hats? Scaring dogs?
I thought I was going to be Max the
Magnificent!'

Sophie stopped and turned to me with a kind smile. 'You'll figure it out, Max, I know you will. You just need to be patient.'

'You sound like my dad,' I said. 'Everyone wants me to be patient. But I need to know **now**! I wonder if the key is finding out more about where the powers came from in the first place.'

'The chest in your gran's shop?' Daisy said.

'Yes,' I replied. 'Arthur Andrews's chest. We need to find out more. Let's go to the shop after my shift on the stall this evening, and we can ask Gran if there's any other stuff she got from his house when he died. Papers, maybe, or photographs.'

'Does she still make those brownies that are all soft in the middle?' Stretch asked, a dreamy look on his face.

'She does,' I said.

'And there'll be tea, right?' he asked anxiously.

'Gallons of it,' I confirmed.

'Then count me in!' said Stretch.

Stretch loves tea.

Car Wars!

Every day after school I head down the market for my shift on the toy stall while Dad goes home for his tea. It's only an hour, and even though it can be hard work, I really enjoy it. It's one of my favourite times of the day, in fact.

Is it because I get to help my family and

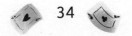

give something back? Maybe a bit.

Is it because I can practise my magic tricks and my stage patter? Maybe a bit.

Is it because I get to show off and attract loads of attention? Yeah. Quite a lot actually.

As soon as Dad has gone, I start my routine. I dance on the tables, I tell jokes, I juggle, I sing songs. Whatever toy Dad wants me to sell, for that hour I give it my all. Sometimes it works out, other times it doesn't. But I **always** have fun and try my hardest.

The only problem is sometimes I get a bit distracted after school. And Dad does **not** like being kept waiting. He wants to go home for his tea.

Today was a day when I was going to be late. Very late. I'd been practising the card trick and time had got away from me. The next thing I knew, it was ten minutes past five and I could hear Dad's rumbling tummy from where I was, half a mile away.

I ran.

If only one of my magical powers was teleportation, I thought. Or time travel. Or Remembering Where I Was Supposed to Be.

'Need a lift?' someone called as I sprinted down the street. I turned my head to see Daisy riding her bike in the cycle lane beside me. Points for riding in the cycle lane, I thought. Points taken away for not wearing a helmet.

'Do I need a lift?' I panted. 'That's like

asking Lucky if he likes sausages. Of **course**
I need a lift.'

'Hop on,' she said.

Daisy's bike has footrests on the back
wheel hub that a passenger can stand on.
You have to hold on to her shoulders. And
when Daisy is riding her bike, you have
to hold on **tight**. Normally I would have
said no; I value my life too highly. But if
I didn't get to the stall in the next few
minutes then Dad was going to kill me
anyway.

I hopped on and immediately regretted
it as Daisy stood on the pedals and powered
us down the street at lightning speed.

'Daisy!' I shouted into her ear. 'You're
seriously messing up my hair!'

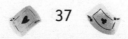

She bunny-hopped onto the pavement and shot across Devonshire Square, scattering pigeons and pedestrians alike.

'You menace!' someone yelled.

'Sorry!' I shouted. We whizzed past Happy Mike. I snatched a coin out of my pocket and tossed it into his hat.

'Thanks, Max Magic!' he sang. 'Hope you don't die!'

Daisy turned sharply into Harrow Place, nearly throwing me off. Round another corner into Middlesex Street, and then we were into Petticoat Lane. She weaved and zipped around the shoppers at breakneck speed. We don't call her Daring Daisy for nothing.

'You can let me off here,' I shouted,

though I wasn't sure she could hear me,
but Daisy carried on right up to the stall.
Dad was standing in front of it, red-faced.
Daisy did a huge screeching turn all the
way around him before coming to a stop.

'Yeehaa!' she whooped.

I hopped off, my heart pounding. I made
the decision there and then to never get on
the back of Daisy's bike again.

'See you tomorrow, Max!' she cried.
Then she was off, nearly clipping the vicar,
who was buying himself a pie.

Dad watched her go, shaking his head.
Then he turned to me. 'You're late!' he
said.

'There was an emergency,' I said,
thinking desperately. 'A fire at school.

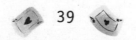

39

I mean, an earthquake. And I got caught up in a search for an escaped tiger. And time got away from me. Anyway, my watch broke and I literally have no way of telling the time.'

Dad frowned.

'Ever heard of the Bow Church clock tower?' he asked.

'Doesn't ring any bells,' I replied, shaking my head.

He sighed. 'Let me guess – you've been practising that magic trick.'

I grinned.

'I'm starting to wish I hadn't shown you,' he said, shaking his head. He turned and walked off towards home.

I felt bad. I know he worked hard,

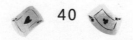

without much reward. Maybe it was time I buckled down and started taking my responsibilities seriously. But I could at least start making it up to him by selling a few toys. I look around and spotted some Spanish tourists talking among themselves by the stall.

'Did you hear about the Spanish magician?' I asked them. 'He counted uno . . . dos . . . then he disappeared without a tres.'

Sometimes when I work on the stall I give myself a little helping hand with a spot of magic. Like today, for instance. Dad had bought a range of remote-controlled

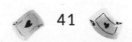

cars, which he was sort of regretting, to be honest, because although they were super-cool, they were quite expensive. People around here don't have a lot of money.

Anyway, I'd set up two cars to chase each other around the stall as I did my patter. One was a police car and the other a bright red sports car. The police car made siren noises and the sports car made revving noises. Anyway, to make

the chase a bit more fun I'd occasionally
make the sports car go up on two wheels,
or the police car would hurtle across
the street and scare the heck out of Mrs
Kumar on the stall opposite. I didn't make
them do anything that you couldn't do
with the controls. But as I wasn't able to
control two cars at the same time as taking
people's money, I used a little magic to
help out.

'My dad bought a new car,' I called out to the passing shoppers, 'one of those Tesla self-driving ones. It parks by itself, it changes lanes without you moving a muscle – it even shouts at cyclists for you.'

With a flick of a finger I made the sports car screech past a couple of mums with little kids, trying to get their attention. The police car followed, its siren wailing, and the kids ran after the cars with a look of delight on their faces.

'They're all made of premium-quality plastic,' I went on. 'We did have some wooden cars once, but they wooden go.' That got a bit of a laugh.

The sports car did a spin and shot off again, the police car in hot pursuit.

'Our new car is quite complicated,' I went on. 'At first Dad couldn't figure out how to fasten the seat belt. But then it clicked.'

A lady came up and asked how much the cars were.

'Ten pounds,' I said, 'or twenty for two.'

She looked slightly confused at that, but reached into her handbag. Temporarily distracted, I accidentally allowed the police car to crash into Mr Gordon's crockery stall. I looked on in alarm as a massive tea set wobbled and looked about to fall. But Mr Gordon managed to grab hold of it just in time. He glared at me. I smiled weakly and made the car drive back to my side of the Lane.

'Dad found a snake on his car the other day. It was a windscreen viper.'

More laughter. People were coming up and inspecting the stacks of cars in their boxes while the sports car and the police car did circles between their legs.

The crowd grew. I was slightly worried PC Peaceful might appear. He didn't like it when too many people congregated in the market. Last time there had been a small riot and, if I'm entirely honest, it was sort of my fault. But things were going too well to stop now. I was grabbing money as people grabbed the boxes of cars.

The crowd was huge now, and I decided I needed to cool things off. I stepped down and concentrated on making sales. Most people were watching the cars, turning their heads as the vehicles went round and round. This was what I loved. This was my destiny, surely. Putting on a show, entertaining the punters.

Then I saw one man in the crowd who wasn't watching the cars. He was watching me.

I was momentarily thrown. He was a short man, wearing jeans and a jacket. There was nothing particularly unusual about him. He had a long thin nose. His face looked pinched and grey. His eyes, though, were bright and sharp and they were pointed firmly in my direction.

I shook my head and carried on. The next time I looked up, the man was gone,

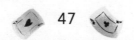 47

and I soon forgot about him. I sold a lot
of the cars, particularly the red sports
car.

'How did you get on?' Dad asked when
he returned with a full belly. 'Shift any
cars?'

'Loads!' I said.

'Brilliant!' he cried. 'Look, Max . . .
about before. I'm sorry I snapped at you.
I was a bit hungry.'

'That's OK, Dad,' I said. 'I'm sorry I
was late. I was practising the trick.'

'One of these days you'll tell me you're
late because you were too busy studying,'
he replied. 'But I'm not holding my
breath.'

I groaned. 'But studying's so boring!'

'Come on, Max,' Dad said. 'There must be some subjects you like?'

I thought for a moment, then shook my head. 'Nope.'

'What about history?

'I don't see the point in history,' I said. 'There's no future in it.'

'Well then, what about science?'

'Me and science? There's no chemistry there.'

'Maths?'

'It just doesn't add up.'

'Geography?'

'Not sure that's the right direction for me.'

'You're good with words, so you must like English?'

I shook my head. 'It doesn't speak my language.'

That finally got a laugh out of him, but then he leaned down and looked me in the eye. 'School is important,' he said. 'You don't have to like it. But you need to take it seriously.'

'I know, Dad,' I said.

He shook his head, grinned and ruffled my hair.

As soon as Sophie, Stretch and Daisy turned up, we set off to Gran's house. I was hoping that Gran had made enough brownies for everyone. I did NOT want to miss out because of the Family Hold Back rule.

But I needn't have worried. It was almost as if Gran had known that I was bringing my friends over as she'd made an extra-big batch. Lucky was going crazy at the smell. Gran always makes a special batch for Lucky using something called carob, because chocolate is bad for dogs.

'Where have you been?!' he cried as I pushed the door open with a tinkle of the little bell.

Gran installed us all in her back room. Stretch had a huge grin on his face. Brownies and tea – this was heaven for him. He and Lucky sat side by side, grinning happily at each other from time to time as they munched. I asked Gran if she could tell us anything more about Arthur Andrews.

 51

'There was an obituary in the local paper a few days after he died,' she said. 'I kept a copy somewhere.' She went off to find it and came back a few minutes later with a copy of the East End Express. 'Here we are,' she said, smoothing the paper out on the old wooden table.

Arthur Andrews

23 April 1933–12 February 2022

Arthur Maurice Andrews was born in Spitalfields in 1933. His father was a soldier and his mother a factory worker. Arthur always loved boats and ships, and when he was fifteen he lied about his age and ran away to sea, joined the merchant navy and sailed the oceans. He returned to the East End every few years to visit his mother, bringing back treasures and curiosities from far-flung parts of the world. He taught himself to read and write and became a renowned expert on many threatened cultures, living with remote tribes in the Amazon jungle, building igloos with the Inuit people of the Arctic Circle and riding ponies across the plains of Mongolia. He had a particular interest in superstition and magical beliefs from around the globe, and wrote a number of articles and books about his findings.

Arthur died leaving no heirs.

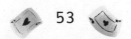

'He loved magic,' Gran said. 'Used to come and see me and your grandad at the Palladium.'

'Apart from the chest,' Sophie asked, 'did he leave anything else?'

'No,' Gran said.

Everyone's shoulders slumped. That wasn't what we wanted to hear.

'Why are you so interested?' Gran asked.

I thought quickly. 'Well, since we found that brilliant top hat in the chest last time, I wondered if there might be any other things that I could use for my stage outfit. You know, a cape, a wand . . .'

'Some better jokes?' Daisy suggested.

'Maybe we should look in the chest again?' Stretch said.

'But we've already looked inside,' Sophie said. 'We know there's just an old suit in there.'

'You never know what you might find when you open an old chest,' Daisy said, winking at me.

Gran said nothing, just watched us all with a faint smile.

'I agree with Stretch,' I said. 'Let's check the chest again. Do you mind, Gran?' I stood up.

'What's the hurry?' Gran said. 'Aren't you going to finish your cup of tea first?'

'There's no time for that!' I said.

'You're wrong, Max,' Stretch said. 'There's always time for tea.'

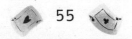

I sat back down, drumming my fingers on the table until everyone had finished. Then I rushed downstairs into the cellar. Lucky and the others followed excitedly.

When I first saw the chest, it was in Gran's back room, but she'd since moved it down into the cellar, which was where she stored all the stuff she wasn't sure what to do with. Old wardrobes and cupboards, cardboard boxes full of papers, faded armchairs. And the chest.

It was under a great big pile of suitcases.

Sophie groaned. 'This will take forever.'

'Wait,' I said. I closed my eyes and let the magical power rise inside me. The pile of suitcases was heavy. A lot of them looked like they might be full.

I took a deep breath and felt the magic grow inside me. Then I used my telekinesis to lift the entire pile and move it over to a bare patch of floor.

'Wow,' Sophie said. 'Sometimes I forget you can do things like that.'

Stretch walked over to the chest and

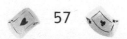

rested a hand on the lid.

'A.A.,' he said slowly, tracing the faded golden letters on the case.

'Those reading lessons are really paying off,' Daisy said, with a mischievous grin.

I stepped forward and took hold of the lid.

'Can I open it?' Stretch said.

I paused, surprised. I hadn't even thought that anyone else might want to try opening the chest. And if they did, I would have expected it to be Daisy rather than Stretch.

'But what if . . . ?' I began. 'What if it happens again?'

Stretch shrugged. 'I guess we'll find out.'

I nodded and stepped back, feeling anxious.

Stretch took a deep breath and opened the lid. We all flinched, expecting a bang and a flash.

Nothing happened.

Part of me was disappointed. A bigger part of me was relieved.

'It's just the suit,' Stretch said, pulling it out.

As he did so, the smell of mothballs and dust puffed out, but there was something else too – an aroma of mysterious spices and perfumes.

'Smells like the timber yard,' Stretch said.

'Smells like my Aunt Jenny's downstairs loo,' Daisy said.

'Smells like the charity shop on the high

 59

street,' Sophie said.

I glared at them. 'You people have no romance in your souls.'

'Wait! What's that?' Sophie said. She was checking the pockets of the suit jacket, and pulled something out.

'It looks like a book,' Daisy said. 'Or a diary.'

'DOOSH!' I said excitedly.

We all leaned in. It was loosely bound in old, stained leather. I opened the cover. The pages were covered with scrawly, spidery writing. It was really hard to read, especially as many of the pages were stained with water, or mould. Some were stuck together.

I thought I could make out a date. 13 February 1956. But the writing was so small and faint it just seemed to wriggle about before my eyes.

'I can't read this,' I said.

'Maybe I should take it home,' Sophie said. 'I could have a go at trying to figure it out.'

I nodded and handed her the book. 'Amazing, thank you, Sophie,' I said,

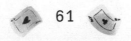

suddenly excited. 'This must be Arthur
Andrews's diary. And maybe it holds the
secret to my magical powers!'

'That's really important to you, isn't it?'
Sophie said, looking at me intently.

'I just feel this diary might help me
figure out why the chest chose me,' I said.
'And what I'm supposed to do now I've got
these powers.'

Back upstairs, Gran was putting up a poster
in the window as Stretch, Daisy and Sophie
left the shop.

'What's that, Gran?' I asked. She turned
and showed me the poster.

Holloughby Productions presents . . .

THE GREATEST SHOW ON EARTH

A nationwide talent show to find the most gifted person in the country!

'**DOOSH!** The most gifted person in the country?!' I cried. 'That's me!'

Gran laughed. 'Well, you don't lack confidence, that's for sure.'

'When you have confidence, anything is possible,' I told her.

'Confidence will get you part of the

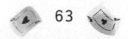 

way, that's true,' she said, 'but you may
need a couple of other things too.'

'Like what?'

'Talent?' she said.

'Tick,' I replied.

'Charm?' she said.

'Tick! Charm is my middle name,' I told
her.

'A willingness to work hard?' she said,
raising an eyebrow.

'Ermmmm. Well, two out of three ain't
bad,' I replied. 'Tell me more about this
competition.'

'There are three categories,' she read.
'Under-18s, Over-18s and Groups. There
are preliminary rounds all over the country,
and then the final will be the winners from

each category, battling for the big prize of £10,000.'

'£10,000!' I exclaimed.

'And the final, to be held at the Globe theatre, will be on television, hosted by the nation's sweetheart, Willow Holloughby,' Gran went on.

'Willow Holloughby!' I gasped. 'I love Willow Holloughby.'

'Everyone does,' Gran agreed. 'She's the nation's sweetheart, says it right here.' She tapped the poster.

'Gran,' I said, 'I am going to enter that competition, and I am going to WIN!'

'Good for you,' she said.

'This is my destiny,' I said, clenching a fist.

 65

'Good-oh,' she said, smiling. 'Hope you've got a good trick planned. Palming coins ain't gonna cut it.'

'Good point,' I said, suddenly brought back down to earth. I had to come up with something big. Something spectacular. And that meant a lot of preparation, practice and . . . patience.

'Unless I . . .' I felt a little tingle in my chest. Could I use my magic – I mean, my **real** magic?

Gran was watching me, a curious look on her face. Then I saw a look of pain cross her face, and she shuffled off to sit in an armchair. Lucky jumped up beside her and she scratched his head.

'Are you all right, Gran?' I asked.

'I'm fine,' she said.
'My hips are playing up
again.'

'Do you want me
to get you a cup of
tea or anything?' I
asked.

'No, no,' Gran
said. 'Look, come and
sit down. I want to tell
you something.'

I perched myself on a
wooden chair next to her. She watched
me carefully, a thin smile on her lovely
wrinkled face.

'There are no shortcuts in life, Max,'
Gran said, as if she'd read my mind.

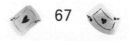
67

'If you want to succeed, you have to put in a bit of captain.'

'Captain?' I asked. Gran often used cockney rhyming slang and I never knew what she meant.

'Captain Kirk, work,' she explained.

'Who's Captain Kirk?'

'Never mind,' she said. 'The point is, you have to put the effort in. The elbow grease. Like your grandad and I did. Like your dad and your mum.'

The light was fading outside, and she reached across to switch on a lamp. Then she turned back to me and grinned her cheeky grin. 'You won't find answers in a chest,' she said. 'You'll find them in your heart.'

I fought the urge to gasp. Did she know about the chest? But maybe it didn't matter. She was right. I knew what she was saying. That I couldn't take a shortcut. I couldn't cheat by using my powers.

'I'll put the work in,' I said.

I left the shop with Lucky soon after, feeling inspired and excited. I'd almost forgotten about Arthur Andrews and the diary. Almost.

As we left, I saw someone looking at the poster in the window of the shop. Someone I recognised. It was the man I'd seen in the market earlier – the short man with the grey face and piercing eyes.

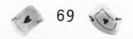 

The man who had been watching me.

He wasn't watching me now though. He was staring at the poster, his eyes even more piercing in the twilight gloom.

There was something about him I didn't like.

I didn't like it at all.

4

Pyramid Panic

For the next few days, after dinner I rushed
up to my room to practise the trick Dad
had shown me. If I was going to win that
competition, I had to be able to perform
lots of tricks like this. So I spent hours
blowing on cards, flicking them out of
sight or flipping them into my sleeve while

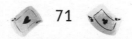

Lucky watched, rolling his eyes and huffing loudly.

On Friday evening he finally managed to persuade me to take him to the park. But I took the Dragonscale cards with me. I sat under a tree by the duck pond practising the trick, while Lucky raced around chasing birds until a goose bit him on the tail and he came running back to me, whimpering.

He switched to chasing pigeons then until we were shouted at by Angry Steve the park-keeper.

After a week of practice, I could sort of do the trick. But it would only work about half the time. The problem was, I found myself getting tense just as I was about to blow on the card. A magician's hands have to be loose and flexible. You have to have confidence and then the magic flows.

I don't know about you, but if I'm ever worried about something, the more I think about it, the worse it gets. But I always think, as long as you try your best, you'll never let yourself down.

I was moaning about it to Mum at breakfast on Saturday morning – about how I felt all jittery and then things went out of control.

'Sounds like you need to get your chi centred,' she said.

'Excuse me?' I replied.

'Your chi,' Mum said. 'It's your life force. I read about it in "Astral Plane" magazine.'

'And it needs to be centred?'

'Yep, it needs to be in alignment with the universe, or else things don't go quite right. But the good news is that you can centre your chi with a bit of meditation. I can show you, if you like?'

I hesitated. Mum was really into spiritual stuff. In the past I would have scoffed at it, like Dad always did. But things were different now. Now I knew that magic was real and there were forces out there that we didn't properly understand, maybe it was time to take Mum a bit more seriously.

'OK, Mum,' I said. 'That would be great.'

She smiled in surprise. 'You won't

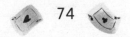

74

regret it, Max,' she said. 'I'll go get the pyramids.'

'The what?'

I sat cross-legged inside my pyramid, hands on my knees, back straight. We were in the sitting room. Mum had assembled two meditation pyramids she'd bought off the internet. When I say pyramids, I mean they were made of eight poles that you put together in a pyramid shape, a bit like a tent but without any canvas.

Then you sit inside the pyramid, for some reason.

She was burning incense. The room was dimly lit by candles and she was playing a

 75

CD called 'Transcendence 2: 24 Soothing Tracks to Recentre Your Chi.'

'Now close your eyes,' Mum said, 'and take a deep breath. Let your soul meld with the universe.'

I closed my eyes. I took a deep breath. And I melded with the universe. I think.

'Can you sense your chi?' Mum asked. 'It should be in your lower spine.'

'I . . . I think so,' I said.

Though it might have been Lucky snuffling around back there.

'Now,' Mum said, 'it's very important that your chi is in alignment with the universe. Otherwise it's like rowing a boat against the current. You have to make sure you're flowing in the same direction as the universe's energy.'

'OK,' I said. I breathed in again, feeling for the chi. And I really think I could feel it. I could see what Mum meant; things weren't in alignment. Something was off

balance. I felt myself correcting, turning, shifting . . .

Then the door opened and Dad came in. 'Oh, great,' he said. 'Now she's got you doing the woo-woo as well.'

And with that, the spell was broken. Mum threw an incense stick at Dad as he left. Then Vinny poked his head around the door. 'Are you two nearly finished in your little tents?' he asked. 'I want to watch Match of the Day.'

'Maybe we should pick this up again tomorrow,' Mum said. 'We can balance your chi then.'

Honestly. How anyone could ever expect to balance **anything** in this house was beyond me.

After dinner on Sunday, I stood up to perform the trick in front of my loving and supportive family.

'Get on with it!' Vinny cried out as I moved chairs aside. He was eyeing up the dessert hungrily. Chris was looking longingly at the scattered bits of his e-bike. Susie was texting. Mum was stacking the dishwasher. Only Dad and Gran were properly watching.

I lit a candle and turned down the lights, to make everything look more atmospheric, and also to make it harder for anyone to actually see what I was doing. That was a little tip I'd picked up from my

favourite magic podcast, 'TrickPod'.

'I've got crumble in the oven,' Mum said. 'How long is this magic show going to take?'

'Just a short spell,' I joked. But no one laughed.

So much for banter.

I shuffled the pack and held it out to Gran. 'Pick a card,' I said, 'any card.'

Gran smiled and plucked a card from the pack. The Jack of Diamonds.

I took the card and held it in my fingers. I felt the familiar tingle in my chest. Gran was watching me very closely, almost as if she knew what I was feeling. But I took a deep breath and pushed the tingle down. Not now, I thought. I was going to do this the old-fashioned way. No cheating!

I felt for my chi. I centred it. The universe was balanced.

I blew sharply on the card.

At that exact moment, Lucky sneezed. Loudly.

The entire universe was knocked off-centre. My chi went for a walk.

The card slipped from my fingers and flew across the room. Everything went into slow motion as the card flipped over and over before landing right on top of the fat red candle in the centre of the table.

POOF!

The plastic-coated card burst into flames and fell onto the tablecloth, which

started to burn. Vinny shrieked. Mum ran to the kitchen, yelling, **'Tea towel, tea towel!'**

Chris grabbed a glass of water and threw it at the blaze, missing entirely. Dad scrambled to his feet but slipped on the spilled water and landed heavily on his bottom with an 'Oof!'

It was Susie who saved the day, grabbing the vase of flowers I'd moved earlier and upending it over the table, extinguishing the flames with a hiss.

'Very good,' Gran cackled. 'Very entertaining.'

I'd remained frozen the whole time, a look of horror on my face. Mum came back in and we all just stood there, looking at the huge black burn in the middle of the table. Apart from Dad, who was still groaning on the floor, rubbing his bottom.

'Excuse me!' Lucky said hotly. 'Isn't anyone going to say bless you?'

Diary and Destiny

The next day at school, Stretch and I
were hanging around by the football pitch,
waiting for Daisy and Sophie and watching
a few kids playing five-a-side. Jamie
Thomson ran up and stopped in front of us.

'Hey,' he said. 'Can you do your thing?'

'No problem,' I said, pulling out a fresh

pack of Dragonscale cards from my pocket.
Dad had replaced the pack with the burnt
card while giving me a lecture about looking
after my possessions.

'Not you, Max,' Jamie said. 'Stretch.'

'Oh yeah,' I said, shoving the cards back
in my pocket. 'I knew that.'

'Sure,' Stretch said with a grin. He
walked over to the wall of the changing-room
block, grabbed hold of an iron drainpipe and
shimmied his way up onto the roof. My mouth
dropped open in surprise. Stretch never
failed to impress. He disappeared from sight.

The football players had assembled
in front of us. They started a low, soft,
'Whooooo . . .' that got louder and louder
until . . .

 85

a football came flying down from the
roof.

The footballers erupted in cheers.
The first ball was followed by a second,
then a third, and a fourth. Ball after ball
came flying off the roof, bouncing onto the
grass, each greeted by a cheer and a round
of applause.

'That's all,' Stretch said, reappearing.
He came about halfway down the drainpipe
and then jumped the rest of the way, doing
a forward roll before hopping lightly to
his feet.

'See you lads next time,' he
said.

'Cheers, Stretch,' Jamie
said as the footballers ran

back to their game.
'They're always losing
balls up there,' Stretch
explained. 'I get them back
once a week or so.'

Sophie and Daisy turned up then.
Sophie was waving a piece of paper at me
impatiently.

'Is that it?' I asked. 'You copied out
the diary?'

'Only a bit of it so far ,' she said. 'Most
was damaged. But I managed to
write out this entry word for
word.' She held it out.

'You read it,' I said.

Sophie smoothed the paper
and began to read.

4 December 1956

I think I have it. The clue I have been
seeking for so long. Yesterday I met
a man who told me a legend about a
magical box that was brought to this
place by a powerful magician many
years ago. The magician disappeared
but left behind him certain items,
including the chest. For that is surely
what it is. The mythical Chest of
Destiny. The item I have spent years
searching for.

I asked the man the whereabouts of
the magical box, and had to part with
a considerable sum before he would
tell me anything more. He told me
of another man, a trader, but warned

me that he would only be found if he wanted to be. He instructed me to seek the trader at night in the market district. So now I must wait until darkness falls, and then I can proceed to the next stage of my quest.

Sophie stopped reading and looked up.

'And then what?' I asked. 'Is that all there was? No more pages?'

'There are,' Sophie said. 'But there's a lot of water damage. It took me hours just to figure this out.'

'We still don't know what the chest does. Where the power comes from,' I said.

Sophie handed the paper back to me and I thanked her.

 89

'Arthur called it the Chest of Destiny,' Daisy said thoughtfully. 'Maybe that's what it does. It helps you to achieve your destiny.'

'You think it gives you whatever you want?' I asked.

'Maybe it doesn't give you what you want. Maybe it gives you what you **need**,' she said.

'I wonder if Arthur Andrews opened the chest?' Stretch mused.

'And did he have powers like yours?' Daisy wondered.

We all looked at each other, but we had no answers. I was sure there was more to discover about the mysterious Arthur Andrews and the Chest of Destiny.

I'd thought there was no way I was going to be able to think about anything but the chest that day, but that was before school assembly. Mr Singh, the drama teacher, got up and told us that there had been so much interest in the Greatest Show on Earth talent show that they were going to run auditions at the school **tomorrow**. Students they thought might be good enough would go through to the proper first round of the competition, and the school would sort out the paperwork and even pay the entrance fee!

Suddenly, it wasn't Arthur Andrews's chest I was thinking about. It was The

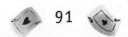

Greatest Show on Earth. And I had to have the Greatest Trick on Earth.

But I didn't have the first clue what that trick was going to be.

Laughs and Lifts

It was the day of the school auditions for
The Greatest Show on Earth. It wasn't
an official round, but the teachers were
weeding out complete no-hopers – and
there were quite a few of those.

Mr Singh would choose the six best acts
and send them through to the first official

round for our region at the town hall on Saturday.

I had been torn between wanting the day to arrive and dreading this moment.

Because I. Had. Nothing.

I'd asked Gran for advice, but she hadn't been much help. She just kept telling me stories about the old days with Grandad and how they'd take turns sawing each other in half. Or locking each other in a wardrobe. I didn't feel confident sawing someone in half, even if I could convince them to let me try. And I could hardly drag a wardrobe up onstage for a three-minute slot. My trick needed to be impressive – and guaranteed not to go horribly wrong in front of my classmates.

I was sitting glumly with my friends in the main hall as a series of students got up and stuttered their way through their acts. There was a clarinet solo, a dance routine and some of the worst jokes I've ever heard.

'I'm gonna need help with my act,' I told the others.

Mr Singh walked past, looking haunted. I liked Mr Singh. He had only started this term, though, and he hadn't yet worked out that at our school every day was a bad day. You just had to roll with it.

'Hello, Mr Singh,' Sophie said brightly.

Mr Singh stopped and looked up. 'Oh, hello, Sophie,' he said.

'How are things going?' she asked.

'It's a disaster.' He groaned. 'No one

has any idea what they're going to do. It's a colossal waste of time.'

Then he saw me. 'Oh, hello, Max,' he said. 'I suppose you're going to do a magic trick, are you?'

'I think he might need some help,' Stretch said. I whacked him on the leg.

'Oh, don't worry,' Mr Singh said. 'I'll find someone to help you. I'm sure your trick will be amazing, Max. You're one of the few I'm not worried about.' With that he hurried off, running his hand through his hair.

'What did you say that for?' I asked Stretch.

'You said you needed help!' Stretch pointed out.

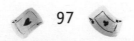 97

'He's right, you did,' Daisy added.

'I meant I need your help to decide what trick I'm going to do,' I said. 'Now Mr Singh thinks I've got some spectacular illusion prepared.'

'Well, haven't you?' Sophie asked.

'No!' I said. 'I've got **nothing!**'

There was a silence.

'What am I going to do?!' I asked.

'What about the Mongolian Rope Trick?' Stretch suggested.

'Where am I going to find a thirty-foot rope, a crossbow and a pony at such short notice?' I sighed.

'Why can't you just do some card tricks?' Sophie said. 'It'll get you through the first round, then you can do something more elaborate for the next stage.'

'I suppose.' I sighed. 'I just wanted to, you know, wow everyone from the start.'

'Seriously, though,' Stretch said, 'you do actually need to do up your laces.'

Then I had a thought. 'Hey, maybe you guys could get up onstage with me and be part of the act! I could bamboozle you with my mind games and you could act all amazed and stuff.'

'We'd love to help,' Daisy said, 'but we have our own acts to prepare for.'

I blinked. 'Um, what?'

'We're all entering the competition too,' Sophie said. 'Didn't you know?'

'You're entering the competition?' I asked, eyes wide. 'What are you doing?'

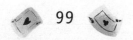

'I'm doing a TED Talk about business opportunities for young adults,' Sophie replied. She held up her Business Book, which is what she calls the notebook that she carries everywhere.

'This is supposed to be a talent show!' I said. 'What talent are you showing off? The ability to send people to sleep?' I winked.

'At least I **have** an act,' she said, winking back. 'Shouldn't you be off somewhere finding a pony?'

While we were bickering, a group of three boys walked onto the stage.

'What's the name of your act?' Mr Singh called out.

'We're called In No Particular Order,' one of them said.

'What? Why?' Mr Singh asked.

'Because when they judge these competitions,' one of the boys replied, 'they always say, "And going through to the next round, in no particular order . . ."'

'Right,' Mr Singh said with a laugh. 'And what's your act?'

'We don't really have one,' the boy said. 'We just thought the name was funny.'

'OK, so in that case, I can tell you who **won't** be going through to the next round,' Mr Singh said. 'In No Particular Order.'

'And what about you?' I asked Daisy. 'What's your act?'

'I'm doing a death-defying jump on my bike over six Year 7s,' she said.

'Death-defying for you or for the Year 7s?' Sophie asked.

'Well, that remains to be seen,' Daisy said grimly. 'It might be them. It might be me. I just don't care. I'm not frightened of **anything**.'

'We have a maths test tomorrow,' Sophie said.

'Oh no!' Daisy said, her face a mask of horror.

I looked at Stretch. He swallowed nervously. 'Please tell me you're with me, Stretch?' I said. 'My old buddy. My bro?'

He shook his head, looking guilty. 'I'm doing a gymnastics display.'

'Well, I gotta say,' I said, 'I really thought you guys would be on Team Max.'

'You can't always expect everyone to drop everything and help you,' Sophie said. 'Other people want to get ahead as well. You're not the only one who wants to achieve things.'

'Well, fine!' I snapped. 'I'll just have to do it by myself.' I stood up and stomped off grumpily.

Then I stopped and came back.

'Sophie, do we really have a maths test tomorrow?'

'Yes,' she said.

'Argh!' I said, throwing up my hands.

I sort of knew I was being unreasonable. Why shouldn't my friends get to enter the

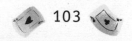

competition for themselves? But I was Max the Magnificent! This was my thing! My destiny! The least my friends could do was help me.

I stormed out of the hall and ran slap bang into a wall, falling back onto my bottom.

Except it wasn't a wall.

It was worse.

It was George Bottley. Bottley the Bully.

I gulped. The last time I'd been this close to George Bottley, things had got out of hand and I'd created an illusion of a giant worm that had tried to choke him. It hadn't been my finest moment.

Bottley reached down and grabbed my

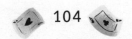

shoulder. I clenched every muscle in my body, expecting to be hurled across the corridor.

But I wasn't hurled anywhere.

Instead, Bottley lifted me up and set me on my feet.

'Sorry,' he said.

I stared at him, sure I must have misheard. 'S-sorry?' I stammered.

'Yes,' Bottley said in his deep voice. 'I'm sorry I knocked you over.'

I shook my head in confusion. What was happening? Was I in a dream?

'Also,' he went on. 'I'm sorry about – well, you know. Taking money off you and flushing your head down the loo and all that.'

 105

My mouth dropped open. Bottley the Bully had just apologised to me! Now I knew it must be a dream.

Just then Mr Singh walked past.'Ah, George,' he said. 'There you are.'

'Here I am,' George replied.

'You said you wanted to do something to help,' Mr Singh went on. 'Well, Max here says he needs help with his magic trick.'

I stared at Mr Singh in amazement. 'You want Bott– um, George to help me?'

'Yes,' Mr Singh said to me. 'George has been attending my drama club for the last few weeks. He says he's not ready to perform himself, but that he wants to help out. That's right, isn't it, George?'

Bottley nodded. He looked at me and

his face did something odd. It took me a
moment, but then I realised he was trying
to smile.

'I'd be happy to help, Max,' he said. 'What's the trick?'

Well, that was a good question. I looked up at him and thought about how easily he'd lifted me just now.

And I knew what my trick was going to be.

Stretch did an amazing routine ending in a double back flip.

Daisy got half a dozen Year 7s to lie down in the middle of the stage then bunny-hopped over all of them on her BMX, to gasps of delight from the children and screams of horror from the teachers.

Sophie came onstage with a headset

and a PowerPoint display and told everyone how they could monetise their social-media platforms without selling out to Big Tech.

Finally it was my turn. I was the last act, and people were starting to get a bit restless, especially after Harriet Norton's mime act in which she spent three minutes standing completely still and later explained she'd been 'stuck in a really small lift'.

'I once did a magic show for a group of mimes,' I said as she walked off. 'They were speechless.'

I reached into my pocket and pulled out the Dragonscale cards. I did a couple of simple card tricks to begin with. I didn't try the trick Dad had shown me, where I

 109

blow on the card to make it disappear. I still wasn't confident with that.

'Actually,' I said, 'I found the previous act quite difficult to watch.'

'So did we!' someone yelled unkindly.

'No, I mean because I'm a bit scared of lifts,' I went on. 'In fact, I've been taking steps to avoid them.'

That got a small laugh.

'You can't trust lifts. Half the time they let you down.' I stepped backwards on the stage. 'I do like jokes about lifts though. They really push my buttons.'

Everyone groaned.

'Sorry.' I grinned. 'These lift jokes are bad on so many levels.'

That got a much better laugh.

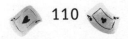

I took another step back. 'It's funny, isn't it, how in America they're called elevators and here in the UK they're called lifts? I guess we're just raised differently.'

Big laugh. I took one more step back and felt the rear curtain brushing against my back. It was time.

'Well,' I said as the curtains at the front of the stage began to close, 'I guess my time is . . . UP!'

And as I said 'Up', I felt a firm hand grab the back of my blazer and hoist me into the air, slowly and smoothly, just like Bottley and I had planned. To the audience, it looked like I was levitating. There was a gasp and a laugh. And

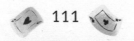 

then the front curtains closed and the thunderous applause started. Bottley let me down and popped out from behind the curtain, a huge grin on his face.

'Did it work?' he asked.

'Listen to the crowd!' I replied, grinning madly. There were cheers, there were whistles, there were cries of 'Encore!' They **loved** us.

'George,' I said, 'I think we're through to the next round.'

Chestnut

When we got into school the next day, we saw a big crowd of students clustered around the main noticeboard.

'Come on,' Stretch said excitedly. 'Let's see if we made it!'

He pushed his way through and scanned the board. 'Yes!' he cried. 'I made it to

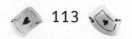 

the next round. You too, Max.'

'Obviously,' I said with a confident grin, though secretly I was relieved.

'What about me and Sophie?' Daisy called over the excited chatter of hopeful students.

But Stretch shook his head. 'Nope, your names aren't on here.'

'Sexism,' Daisy spat.

'Anti-capitalist bias,' Sophie added. 'I think we should appeal.'

'I agree,' Daisy said, and the girls marched off towards Mr Singh's room. However badly his day was going, it was about to get much worse, I thought.

'So we're officially going to the first proper round at the town hall!' Stretch said.

We looked at each other and bumped fists.

'May the best man win,' Stretch said.

'Thanks,' I said.

'You seem very pleased with yourself,' Lucky said as I arrived at Gran's shop after my shift that evening.

'I'm through to the first proper round of the talent show,' I explained.

'Well done,' said Gran, entering the shop from the back room. I think she assumed I was speaking to her. I mean, why would I be talking to a dog, right?

'What trick did you do?'

'Levitation,' I said.

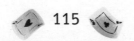 115

'Goodness!' she exclaimed.

I explained how I'd done it, with Bottley's help.

'Bottley?!' Lucky shouted in shock.

'Stop barking, you old fleabag,' Gran said. 'Isn't Bottley the bully?'

'Yeah, but he seems to have turned over a new leaf,' I said. 'He even apologised.'

Lucky and Gran looked at each other. Then a customer approached the counter and Gran went off to help. I noticed she was hobbling a little. Poor old Gran. I wished I had a magic power that could make her hips feel better.

'Come on, Lucky,' I said when she'd gone. 'I want to check the chest again. Just in case.'

'You've already checked it twice,' he pointed out.

'Yeah, and the first time we missed the diary altogether. Maybe we missed something the second time. I'm going to see if there are any more pockets in that suit.'

'I don't trust Bottley,' Lucky said, as we went downstairs.

'You don't trust anyone,' I pointed out. 'You think our postman is a serial killer.'

'He fits the profile,' Lucky growled.

'Maybe people can change,' I said. 'I think we need to give Bottley a chance.'

I clicked on the light in the cellar, and after a brief look around I saw the chest under a pile of old sheets and blankets.

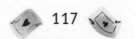 117

I moved them to one side and ran my fingers across the gold lettering on the top of the box.

A.A.

This time I didn't really expect anything to happen when I lifted the lid. After all, nothing had happened to Stretch. I thought I'd see the old dark suit lying there, folded up, just as we'd left it a couple of days before.

But something did happen.

There was a **BANG.**
And there was a **FLASH.**

And the next thing I knew, I was lying on the other side of the room.

This time I'd managed to avoid bumping my head at least, but my shoulder whacked against a heavy old cupboard, causing a shower of dust to fall on my head and shoulders.

I coughed.

'Oh no,' Lucky said. 'Not again.'

I hadn't really thought that the chest might work twice. But when I sat up and blinked, I felt the familiar tingle in my chest and my head was swimming, just like before.

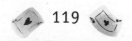

Lucky was watching me suspiciously.

'I think it's given me a new power,' I whispered. 'I can feel something fluttering inside me. Something new.'

'What now?' He sighed. 'Can you fly? Can you see the future? Can you make bacon appear out of thin air?'

'Dunno,' I said. 'I'm hoping it's fireballs. Or lightning bolts.'

I lifted my arm.

Lucky yelped and dived behind the pile of suitcases. 'Not here!' he barked.

'Good point,' I said. 'Come on, let's go to the park and see if I can blow something up.'

'Well, it's not fireballs,' Lucky said. 'Or lightning bolts.'

I'd been trying to blow up some soft-drink cans for the last fifteen minutes. We were in a quiet corner of the park and keeping a close watch out for anyone approaching. I certainly didn't want Angry Steve the park-keeper to see me do magic. That would be hard to explain. But even if he was watching, he wouldn't have seen anything, because no matter how much I pointed my arm and tried to visualise fire or lightning coming out of my fingertips, nothing happened.

I'd tried saying, **'Abracadabra!'**
I'd tried saying, **'Hey presto!'**
I'd tried saying, **'DOOSH!'**

But nothing worked.

I could still do the telekinesis, of course. And my other powers.

But I wanted something dramatic. Something like fireballs.

'Can we go now?' Lucky said. 'I'm hungry.'

I sighed. I supposed I'd have to try again tomorrow. Maybe I didn't have a new power? Maybe I'd just got a recharge, like in a video game. If only Sophie could translate more of Arthur Andrews's diary, maybe we'd find some answers in there.

As we walked toward the park gate, Lucky started complaining about Wacky Dog again.

'I saw the can your mum has ready

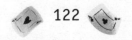

for me tonight,' he grumbled. 'It's just named "Meat". Not even identifiable as any particular species. Just general "Meat and meat-adjacent products".'

'Oh, for heaven's sake.' I sighed. I was still feeling the magic tingle in my chest, and it was a little distracting. 'I suggest you stop complaining about Wacky Dog and just learn to enjoy it.'

'OK,' Lucky said immediately.

I stopped walking. He carried on for a few steps, then turned around to look at me.

'What?' I said.

'What?' he said.

'Did you just agree to do what I asked?'

Lucky shrugged, which isn't an easy

thing for a terrier to do, but he managed it somehow. 'Well, yeah. It's the only sensible thing to do. I need to stop complaining and just learn to like Wacky Dog.'

'You've never done anything I've suggested before,' I pointed out.

'Well, you've never suggested anything sensible before,' Lucky said, then he turned and trotted off.

When we got home, the house was in even more chaos than usual. Dad was still not home, so Mum was cooking and washing up and setting the table, which was difficult because Chris had spread the various bits of his e-bike all over it. Susie was in the messy sitting room, her feet up, talking loudly on her phone. Vinny was watching a football

match on his iPad and
shouting at the ref.

Mum rolled her
eyes at me. 'They
won't do anything
I ask,' she said.
'It's easier to do it
myself, otherwise I spend
the whole evening shouting.'

Now, if I'm totally honest, I can't
pretend that I'm the most helpful son
in the world. I've been known to leave
the occasional mouldy sandwich in my
room, or spill milk in the fridge and not
wipe it up, and I could guess where the
washing machine is but I couldn't be
100% certain. But even I could see my

siblings were taking the biscuit here.

'Chris,' I snapped, 'how about you clean up all this e-bike mess? Vinny, why don't you help me set the table? Susie, maybe it's time to get off the phone and clear up the sitting room?'

'OK,' they chorused.

I blinked in astonishment as Chris began tossing all the bike parts into a box. Vinny turned off his football game and went to get some knives and forks. Susie said goodbye to her friend and started tidying the sitting room.

None of my siblings had **ever** done anything I asked before.

'OK,' Mum said slowly. 'That's weird, but I'm not going to complain.'

My mind was racing. This wasn't normal. Not just in our house, but in anyone's house. No youngest child has ever been listened to by their own family in the history of the human race.

I looked over to see Lucky happily wolfing down a big bowlful of Wacky Dog.

'Something strange is going on,' I muttered.

All in the Mind

'Is this my new power?' I asked the next day as the gang and I were walking into school.

'So let me get this straight,' Sophie said. 'All you did was suggest something, and they all just did it straight away, without arguing?'

'That's right,' I said.

Sophie knew Lucky, and she's met my family. She knew how odd this was.

'Mind control,' she said. We'd reached school now and were sitting on a bench by the playground. Stretch was on the monkey bars, doing flips.

'What?'

'It's the power of mind control,' Sophie said. 'Have you ever seen a hypnotist making people quack like a duck or miaow like a cat?'

'Of course,' I said. 'But that's not **real** magic.'

'I think that's what you've got,' Sophie said. Then she narrowed her eyes and pointed a finger at me. 'Try it on me.

But don't make me do anything dangerous or embarrassing.'

'Would I do that?' I protested. 'OK, how about you sit next to me in maths and share your answers in the test today?'

'OK,' Sophie said straight away.

'What?!' Daisy said. 'You'd do that?!'

'Sure,' Sophie said. 'But that's a reasonable request. You need to ask me to do something I would normally say no to.'

'Sophie,' Daisy said, 'you have never cheated in your life. You **hate** cheating.'

Sophie looked puzzled.

'Sophie, how about you forget what I just said about the test?' I said.

'OK,' Sophie said. 'Now, are you going to suggest something for me to do?'

I looked up at Daisy, who said to Sophie,
'How about you sit next to Max in maths
and let him see your answers to the test?'

'Are you crazy?!' Sophie shouted.
'That's the most ridiculous idea I've ever
heard.'

'I think that settles it,' I said. 'I have
the power of mind control. I can make
people do what I suggest to them, and

they'll think it's the most reasonable thing in the world.'

'You can make people do things for you,' Daisy said.

'I don't want people to do things for me,' I said.

'I don't get why you're not more excited,' Daisy said. 'This is a really cool power.'

'I suppose it is,' I said, frowning. 'It's also the sort of power that could get me into a lot of trouble.'

Then the bell rang, and we set off towards the school buildings.

'Wait,' Sophie called. 'Aren't you going to suggest something?'

'Max,' Stretch said as he walked beside

me, 'do you think if I opened the chest again, I might get magical powers this time?'

'I don't know,' I said. 'Maybe it only works for me.'

'Maybe,' he said. 'Or maybe it only works sometimes – like, randomly.'

'Hmm,' I said. 'I suppose it's possible.'

'Maybe we should try it,' he said.

'Maybe,' I replied. I stopped and turned to face him. 'Are you sure you'd want that though? Having these powers is . . . Well, it's . . .'

'It's what?' Stretch asked.

'It's . . . confusing,' I said. 'All I know is, ever since I went down into the basement under Gran's shop and opened

133

that chest, my life has been a lot more complicated. It's useful to be able to move heavy boxes around, and I love being able to talk to Lucky. But I have to be careful what I do with my powers. It's easy to let things get out of control. Remember that time I made Bottley eat a giant worm?'

'I do.' A deep voice came from behind me. I spun around to see Bottley himself.

'Oh,' I stammered. 'Hello, B– er, George.'

How much had he heard?

'I put a few worms in your mouth too,' he said with a little grin. 'Lots of little ones rather than one big one. Let's call it even.'

'Oh. Ha ha. Yeah, sure,' I said. My

mind was racing, trying to remember
exactly what I'd said to Stretch about the
chest.

'One day I'll work out how you did
that . . . trick, Max Magic,' he said with
a wink. Then he walked off.

'I still don't trust that guy,' Stretch
said as we walked towards our classroom.

'You need to give him a chance,' I
said. 'He's changed. And he's genuinely
sorry for the way he used to be.'

'I don't think people like that change,'
Stretch said. 'Not really.'

Bottley had been so nice and helpful
over the last week or so. The change
in him did seem genuine. But there had
been something in his tone just now

 135

that I hadn't liked. Almost like he knew something. What an idiot I'd been to talk about my powers in public!

I hoped it wouldn't come back to haunt me.

9

Stop the Press!

That evening, when I went to see Gran, she passed me a plate of cookies and we sat and ate them together.

'There was a bloke sniffing around the shop yesterday,' she said. 'Asking a lot of questions, he was. Turned out he's a reporter from the East End Express, but at

first I thought he might be ducks.'

I shook my head in confusion. 'Ducks? Is that more rhyming slang?'

'Ducks and geese,' she said. 'Police. Thing is, he was asking about you.'

'Me?' I said, surprised. My tummy dropped. What would a reporter want with me? 'What did he want?'

'Well,' Gran said, 'he asked a lot of questions about that big storm we had, when the Crayfish Twins were arrested. He seemed to think you had something to do with it.' She peered at me closely.

'What would I have had to do with it?' I asked.

She stared at me in that knowing way, then smiled. 'Dunno. Anyway, I thought I should tell you. I'd keep clear of him if I were you.'

Then the bell at the shop door tinkled so she shuffled off, wincing and rubbing her hip.

'Thanks, Gran,' I called after her.

Lucky had been listening to the whole thing but had kept quiet. When she'd gone though, he spoke. 'Maybe you should talk to this reporter,' he said.

'Why?'

'Well, you'd get your name in the papers: **Crayfish Twins Arrested as Hero Boy Max Saves Market.**'

I nodded. If I was going to be Max the Magnificent, I'd need the press on my side. And once I'd won The Greatest Show

on Earth, the papers were going to be all over me anyway. I'd be doing interviews on all the big TV shows and turning on the Regent Street Christmas lights. There'd be limousines and private jets and helicopters probably.

But then I remembered the look in the man's eyes as he had watched me in the market. There was something about him I really didn't like.

'I think I might save my story for one of the big papers,' I said. 'We're on the up, you and me. And then you can eat all the Waggy Boy you like.'

'And stop eating Wacky Dog?' Lucky said, aghast. 'No fear. Oh, and I suppose your new friend Bottley will be coming with

us in our majestic rise to the top?' Lucky
sounded sarcastic.

'Of course,' I said. 'He's literally the
one lifting me up.'

'The wind beneath your wings,' Lucky
said.

'Something like that,' I said.

'Are you sure you can trust him?' Lucky
asked, looking dubious.

'I'm pretty sure I can,' I said. But then I
remembered that he'd overheard me talking
to Stretch about the chest, and I felt a chill
run up my spine.

'Who can you trust?' Gran asked, walking
back in.

'Bottley,' I said. 'At least, I think I can.
Do you think people can change, Gran?'

 141

She sat and looked thoughtful for a moment, then she nodded. 'I used to know this bloke, theatre owner. Horrible man. Shouted at his staff. Fired people and refused to pay them. He hated animals – and you should never trust someone who doesn't like animals. Never looked after the theatre either – rats running everywhere, the whole place was cream-crackered.'

'Knackered?' I asked.

'You're getting the hang of it,' Gran said. 'Anyway. One day he'd had too much to drink and only went and fell in the Thames, didn't he? Couldn't swim a stroke. There he was, splashing and trying to call out. As he was going down for the third time, he feels a big hand grab his collar and someone hauls him out of the river.'

'Close call,' I said.

'Yeah, and the strange thing was, the bloke wouldn't take any credit. Wouldn't even give his name. The theatre owner wanted to give him a reward, but the stranger wouldn't hear of it. He said that anyone would have done the same thing, then went off into the night.'

'Wow,' I said. 'Like a superhero.'

'Exactly,' Gran said. 'Anyway, from that day on, the theatre owner was a changed man. He paid everyone promptly, stopped shouting, and he got himself a little cat to clear out the rats from the theatre.'

'So people **can** change,' I muttered thoughtfully.

 143

'Yep,' Gran said. 'Some people just need a chance to be able to change, and a little support along the way. Sometimes you need to show them what's right, and what's wrong.'

10

Judgement Day

At breakfast the next day, I saw I had an email from the competition organisers. The heading read:

'Meet the Judges!'

'The second round will have three celebrity judges!' I said, reading the email aloud at the breakfast table. 'And I'll get to meet them.'

'You have to get through the first round first,' Mum pointed out.

'That won't be a problem,' I said.

'So,' Susie said, very excited, 'who are the judges?'

Dad rolled his eyes. I knew what he was thinking. He wasn't a big fan of celebrities. It's just showing off, he always says. Vinny didn't seem interested either. He was reading a football magazine, paying no attention.

'Judge 1 is Shussy D,' I read out. 'Singer, dancer, YouTuber, producer and influencer.'

'Shussy D?!' Susie exclaimed. 'She's so cool! She has over a hundred thousand followers on AppSnap.'

'Well, I've never heard of her,' Dad
said, folding his arms.

'Well, no, but that's because you're,
like, nearly seventy.' Susie rolled her eyes.

'I'm forty-eight!' Dad exclaimed.

'Exactly,' Susie said. 'Nearly seventy.'

Susie is even worse at maths than I am.
And that's saying something. I hadn't had

my maths test result back, but let's just say
I wasn't feeling confident about it.

'I haven't heard of her either,' I
admitted.

'Well, let me assure you,' Susie said,
nodding her head vigorously, 'Shussy D is
going places, and one day soon **everyone**
will have heard of her.'

'You should try to get a selfie with her,
Max,' Mum said.

'She should try to get a selfie with me,
you mean,' I said.

'Who are the other judges?' Mum asked.

'Judge 2: Fox Blackshaw,' I said.

'Never heard of him either,' Dad said
immediately.

'Ooh,' Mum said. 'I like him.'

'Is he the guy who ate the snake in the desert on that survival programme?' Chrissy asked. 'Extreme Outback Bivouac?'

'He's very rugged,' Mum said dreamily. 'I'd go on an extreme bivouac with him.'

'And who's the third judge?' Chrissy asked.

I looked down at the page. 'Willow Holloughby of course!'

'Willow Holloughby?' Dad said, pricking up his ears.

'Oh, **now** you're interested,' I said.

'Well,' Dad said, 'she's the nation's sweetheart.'

Sophie messaged the group as I walked

 149

to school, telling us to meet her at the churchyard.

'I've transcribed some more of Arthur Andrews's diary,' she said once we were all there. 'And it's **very** interesting.'

She showed me a page in her Business Book.

'You read it,' I said, my heart pounding.

'Yes, go on,' Daisy said. 'Read it, Soph.'

Sophie took a deep breath and started to read.

If the shopkeeper in the market is to be believed, the chest is over 400 years old. It was created by a powerful magician and the tale mostly fits with my research. All those months of surrounding myself with dusty tomes in dark, stuffy rooms in the British Library seem to have paid off.

The chest sits in my room now, brooding. It is locked and I do not wish to damage it by forcing the catch. The shopkeeper had no key. Tomorrow I will find a locksmith who can open it for me.

I sit here in candlelight, listening to the calls of the fruit vendors in the street below, and I watch the chest.

What rests within? Or should I say, WHO rests within?

'Whoa,' Daisy said. 'This is awesome!'

'What did he mean when he said **who**

151

rests within?' Stretch said. 'Was there someone trapped in the chest?'

'I don't know,' Sophie said. 'That's all there was on the page. I flicked forward a few pages and I think there are some other parts that I should be able to figure out. I'm getting better at interpreting the handwriting. But it still takes ages.'

'You're doing a great job,' I said. 'Sorry if it sounds like I'm being impatient. I just know the secret of the chest is in there somewhere.'

'Thanks,' Sophie said. 'Now come on, we'll be late.'

When I got to school, thoughts of Arthur Andrews and the chest were soon replaced by talk of The Greatest Show on Earth.

The competition was pretty much all anyone talked about that day. I tend to get a little overexcited sometimes, but this was like nothing else. I was buzzing like a bumblebee. I had to practise my breathing to try to balance my chi, like Mum had shown me. That helped me calm down a bit.

'This is going to be amazing,' I told Lucky as we walked home that night after I'd collected him from Gran's. 'Everything is going to change. This is my **destiny!**'

But destiny had other ideas for me, it seemed. When I got home Mum and Dad were sitting at the kitchen table looking serious. Dad must have closed up the stall early.

 153

'Hello?' I said, a knot forming in my stomach. This didn't look good.

'Max,' Mum said, 'we got a call from school today, about your maths test.'

My heart dropped to my boots.

'Let me guess,' I said. 'I aced it! They want me to be Professor of Sums at Oxford University!'

Mum shook her head.

'Cambridge?'

'Max, this isn't funny,' Dad said. 'You got the lowest score in the class.'

'Oh,' I said. I thought I hadn't done very well, to be fair, but the lowest score in the class?

'Max,' Dad said, 'we're not angry. We just want you to do the best you can. And I think this is as much my fault as yours.'

'Your fault?' I asked, puzzled.

'I showed you that magic trick the other day,' he said, 'and told you to go and practise it. That's why you didn't have any time to study.'

'No,' I said, suddenly worried about where this was heading. 'I have time, I just was being lazy. I'll do better from now on, I promise.'

'We know you will,' Mum said. 'But we have to do our bit as well, help you manage your time better. So you won't be working on the stall any more until the holidays.'

'But I love working on the stall!' I cried.

'And we want you to pull out of the talent show,' Dad said.

'Excuse me?' I said, staring at him. 'It sounded like you just said you wanted me to pull out of the talent show.'

'Yes,' they chorused.

'The Greatest Show on Earth,' I said.

'The greatest waste of time on Earth,' Dad said sternly.

'You can't be serious?!' I cried. 'That's not fair.'

'Max,' Dad said, sighing, 'there'll be plenty of time for magic, and for working, when you've finished school. But for now you need to focus on your schoolwork, OK?'

I went up to my room after that and lay on my bed. Lucky nuzzled into my armpit. I felt like crying. And if I'm honest, I did cry a bit. Well, a lot. It was so frustrating.

I'd been so close to being Max the Magnificent.

Willow in da House

I don't know quite how she managed it, but Sophie persuaded Mr Singh to put Daisy through to the first round of The Greatest Show on Earth. I expect it involved persistence, logical arguments and a threat to move to a different school. Sophie is the smartest person in our school. If she left, the Department for Education would probably send an inspection team around to put us in special measures. Daisy did have to sign a document promising to abide by all the requirements of the Health and Safety in Schools and Public Places Act (1974).

I was miserable about not being able to carry on in the competition myself. But I was happy for Daisy.

So, on Saturday, we found ourselves at the town hall for the auditions for the first proper round. Even if I wasn't allowed to take part, I wanted to go and support my friends.

I'd sent a message to Bottley telling him that I had to pull out of the competition.

I was very apologetic and made it clear my parents were the villains here. He didn't respond. I hoped he wasn't too disappointed.

The way the competition worked was everyone got three minutes, after which a team of bored-looking non-celebrity judges would make a note on a piece of paper and say, 'Thank you. Next.' Then at the end of the day they'd make you go into two different rooms and tell you if you were through or out.

At first it was really exciting. Stretch was having the time of his life. There was a massive refreshments table with over a hundred different types of tea and he was working his way through them one by one,

making tasting notes on a page torn out of
Sophie's Business Book.

But then we all just sat around waiting.
Me, Daisy, Stretch. Mr Singh came by at
one point to make sure we were OK.

'Daisy,' he said, 'please tell me you're
not going to endanger the lives of any Year
7s today.'

'OK,' Daisy said carefully. 'I'm not
going to endanger the lives of any Year 7s
today.'

Mr Singh opened his mouth as though he
was going to ask a follow-up question. But
then we were interrupted by the arrival of
Bottley.

'Bot– George?' I said, surprised. 'What
are you doing here?'

He looked puzzled. 'I'm here for the auditions,' he said.

'Didn't you get my message?' I asked.

He looked at his phone, then groaned.

But before he could say anything, the double doors were flung open and someone walked in, surrounded by a retinue of people holding bags and coffee cups, make-up kits and cameras.

'Willow Holloughby!' Mr Singh said, gulping.

'*DOOSH!*' I said.

And then something extraordinary happened. Willow Holloughby walked right up to our little group. Maybe it was because we were standing in the middle of the room and were the first people she saw.

Or maybe it was destiny.

'Hello there!' she said, then gave us one of her dazzling smiles. 'Are you all in the competition?'

Mr Singh was tongue-tied. He made a strangled sound.

'I'm not,' Sophie said. 'But Daisy here is doing an incredible bike stunt, and Stretch has a fantastic acrobatics show.'

'Amazing. I can't wait to see them,' Willow said. 'And you?' She looked at me and Bottley.

'Unfortunately we can't . . .' Bottley began.

'. . . we can't tell you what our act is going to be,' I interrupted smoothly. 'But it's going to be **unbelievable!**'

'Ooh, very mysterious,' Willow said. 'Does it have anything to do with the top hat you're wearing?'

'You'll just have to wait and see.' I winked at her.

She laughed and went off to talk to some of the other contestants, her assistants following like a gaggle of geese.

'What's going on?' Bottley said. 'First you tell me the act isn't going ahead, then it is.'

'We haven't officially pulled out yet,' I

said. 'We can't stop now Willow Holloughby is going to be watching. This is my big chance. This is destiny. I can feel it!'

'But what about your dad?' Sophie asked. 'Won't he be cross?'

'Well, he doesn't have to know,' I said.

'But what if you win?' Daisy said. 'What if you get to the final and go on telly? He's probably going to figure things out once he sees you pop up on Saturday night TV next to Ant and Dec.'

'We'll cross that bridge when we come to it,' I said impatiently.

Just then, an enthusiastic lady with a headset, a clipboard and a ponytail bounced up to us. 'I need Stretch!' she said brightly.

We all looked over at the refreshments table, where Stretch was making himself another cup of tea.

'That's me,' Stretch shouted. He put his cup down with a look of regret, then came bounding over. 'Do I have time for a wee? I've drunk a lot of tea today.'

'No, not really,' the clipboard lady said.

'OK,' he said as the clipboard lady led him off. 'In that case I might leave out the bit where I do the splits.'

'Go for it, Stretch!' Daisy cried.

'You'll smash it!' Sophie called.

'Break a leg,' I yelled. Then as an afterthought, 'Not literally!'

A few minutes later, we watched on a screen as Stretch did his amazing gymnastics

routine. He'd added a new bit at the end
where he ran up a wall, did a flip and landed
on his feet.

The judges grinned and scribbled furiously
on their pads. I nodded.

'He's through, don't you think, George?
As long as he doesn't mess up the next . . .'
I paused. 'George?'

But Bottley had gone. I looked around the
big, busy room. Maybe he'd gone to the loo.

'What's he doing?' I heard Sophie say. I
looked back at the screen, but Stretch had
disappeared.

'He just ran off halfway through his act,'
Sophie said. 'Oh, there he is!'

Stretch came sprinting past us
and crashed through the toilet doors.

 167

'Emergency!' we heard him yell. I looked back at the screen. The judges were shaking their heads.

'Well, that's the end of Stretch,' Daisy said. 'He didn't get around to doing the triple back flip. That was his showstopper.'

I looked around the room again. Willow had gone to join the judges at the table in the next room. But I did see Bottley. Talking to someone.

Someone familiar. Someone thin, with a grey, pallid expression and piercing blue eyes.

The reporter!

'What's he doing here?' I asked Sophie. She looked over.

'To be fair, Max,' she said, 'he **is** a

reporter, and this is the sort of thing a local reporter might want to write a story about. It is The Greatest Show on Earth, after all.'

'Yes, I suppose you're right,' I said. But just then the reporter and Bottley turned to look at me. They stopped talking, then turned away again. My heart sank.

'Uh oh,' I said.

At that point I was distracted by Daisy being summoned to the auditorium. She had been very secretive about exactly what she was planning, and I'd noticed she'd been carefully avoiding Mr Singh. A couple of assistants in black T-shirts rushed into shot, carrying a ramp. They placed it on the carpet in front of the judges.

'That can't be right,' Sophie said. 'The ramp is facing the judges' table. They must have made a mistake.'

Suddenly, as we watched, Daisy burst out from between the curtains at the far end of the room on her bike. She pedalled furiously, a look of determination on her face. She hit the ramp at an incredible speed and flew into the air. The camera angle switched to show the judges looking up in terror as Daisy's bike sailed over them, missing their heads by centimetres. If the guy in the middle hadn't ducked, she would have taken him out. Daisy landed heavily and slid around in a great skidding sweep, leaving tyre marks on the carpet. She raised a fist and whooped in triumph.

'You should have seen your faces,' she yelled.

'You're out!' the three judges roared. Willow just sat there with a look of horror on her face.

Mr Singh groaned.

'Max Mullers?' a voice said beside me.

I turned to see the reporter staring at me with those intense eyes. I instinctively took a step back. When it comes to my mind-reading power, I'm careful not to go poking around inside people's minds the whole time. It's just rude. And to be honest, sometimes people are thinking about things that are kind of weird. But right now, I was tempted. I really needed to know what this man wanted from me.

'My name is Michael Lewis,' he said.
'I'm with the East End Express.'

I knew the East End Express. Dad
brought it home sometimes. Most of its
stories seemed to be about crime and
disorder and how awful children are these
days. But Dad had brought me up to always
be polite. I held out my hand. 'Pleased to
meet you,' I said.

Michael smiled and shook my hand.
'What a polite young man you are,' he said.
'So unusual these days.'

'I don't think so,' I said. 'Most
young people are polite and kind, in my
experience. Often it's the older generation
who are angry and selfish.'

'Perhaps you're right,' Michael said,

raising an eyebrow. 'Are you excited about the competition?'

'I'm excited about **winning**,' I said with a grin. 'I'm excited about being on TV and receiving a prize of £10,000 from Willow Holloughby.'

He nodded. 'You know, once I was due to appear on a television programme with Willow Holloughby.'

'Really?' I asked.

'Yes. I won a competition, rather like this one,' he said.

'Amazing!' I said. 'Good for you!'

Then he frowned. 'But it got cancelled at the last minute,' he said, an edge of irritation in his voice. 'Apparently the ratings weren't good enough.'

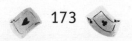 173

'Oh, I'm sorry to hear that,' I said. Why was this man even here? I thought. What did he want with me?

'If only I hadn't missed that chance, my life could have been very different,' he said. 'Do you ever feel that, Max? That you just get one shot? And if you blow it . . . well, that's it.'

'But you're a reporter for the East End Express,' I said. 'That's a really cool job. Meeting loads of people. Writing stories, exposing corruption, and holding politicians to account!'

'Pah,' Michael said, shaking his head. 'All they want are stories about young people shoplifting and hanging around the supermarket like a bad smell. The paper isn't interested in exposing the real crooks. I have loads of ideas, but no one ever listens to me.'

'I'm sorry,' I said. I didn't know what else to say. Again I wondered what all this was about. Why was he so interested in me?

'Anyway,' he went on, 'you seem very confident that you're going to win this competition.'

'I **know** I'm going to win,' I said. I knew I was boasting, but confidence is half the battle. If you're confident, anything is possible!

'How do you know that?' the man asked. 'Do you have some kind of . . . secret weapon? Some special power?'

I looked at him in alarm. What did he

 175

know? Had Bottley said something to him? Why had he been sniffing around Gran's shop? Why had he been asking about the windstorm in the market?

'N-no,' I said. 'I'm just going to try my best, and hope that–'

'Max Magic!' the lady with the clipboard shouted. 'You're up!'

'Gotta go,' I said to the man, and rushed off, relieved. But just before I went through the curtain to the judges' room, I looked back. Michael Lewis was still watching me.

Bottley joined me and gave me an encouraging nod. I wanted to ask him what he'd been talking to the reporter about, but now wasn't the time. I took a deep breath and pushed my way through to the stage, leaving Bottley hidden behind the curtain.

As soon as I was standing there before the judges, seeing Willow Holloughby's winning smile, with the bright lights shining down on me, I felt at home. All the doubts disappeared. I even forgot about Michael Lewis.

I reached into my pocket and pulled out my trusty pack of Dragonscale cards.

'I come from a family of failed magicians,' I began. 'I have two half-sisters . . .'

The show was perfect. The judges laughed at most of my jokes, and Willow kept

 177

nodding in encouragement. Bottley's hand snaked through the curtain and lifted me smoothly and invisibly at exactly the right time, and the judges gasped in amazement. They all scribbled away in their notebooks, grinning and nodding at each other. Willow nodded and gave me a thumbs up.

'I think we're through,' Bottley said to me afterwards, and gave me a high five that nearly knocked me over.

'I saw you talking to that reporter guy,' I said as we wandered over to the refreshments table. 'What did he want?'

'Oh, nothing really,' Bottley said, shrugging. 'He was just asking questions about the competition, you know. Hey, they have Choco Rolls!' He grabbed a handful of snacks, jammed them into his mouth and walked off. Somehow I had the feeling he had deliberately changed the subject.

Daisy, Stretch and Sophie came over.

'You were brilliant!' Daisy cried.

'That was even better than the show at the school,' Stretch said.

'I think you can do better,' Sophie said.

'Thanks for the words of encouragement, Soph,' I said.

Mostly I was delighted to have a good chance of going through to the next round. But at the same time I was worried about Mum and Dad finding out. If I got through, it made the problem more immediate. Was I going to have to lie to him?

'I just think it seems too obvious that you're being lifted,' Sophie was saying. 'Because you have to walk back and stand right in front of the rear curtain. If there was a way that Bottley could be further forward without being seen, that would make the trick even more impressive.'

'Sounds good,' I said, nodding. 'Do you know a way of doing that?'

'No,' she said. 'But I bet your gran does.'

'DOOSH!' I said. 'Great idea! I'll ask her about it when I see her tomorrow. I wonder if I should get Bottley along to talk to her as well.'

Sophie pulled a face. 'You want to

 180

introduce Bottley the Bully to your gran?'

'I couldn't do the trick without Bottley,' I pointed out. 'And he's changed. Isn't it odd how he's gone from being the absolute worst person to being so helpful?'

'It is odd. Too odd,' Sophie said. 'I don't trust him. He's gone from being terrifying to being shifty.'

'And he smells like fish,' Daisy said.

'And he supports Arsenal,' Stretch added.

'I can't believe you guys are being so mean to him,' I said. 'Have you never heard of giving someone a second chance?'

'He's had plenty of chances,' Daisy said. 'He used most of them to stuff your head down the toilet.'

181

'Remember last year?' Stretch said. 'When he made you stand in the middle of the park until he'd gone home. You were so worried he'd see you leave that you stood there until it was dark.'

'He's **changed**,' I said crossly. 'Do you not know what "changed" means? And he joined Team Max when you guys didn't want to. So maybe **you** need to get used to the fact that he's going to be around **permanently**.'

'Fine,' Sophie snapped. 'I hope you and Bottley have a lovely time together.' Then she turned and walked off. Daisy and Stretch followed her.

We did have a lovely time, as it happened.
Well, maybe not lovely. But it was fine.
Bottley and I hung around to watch some
of the entrants from the other categories.
Most of them weren't that great, but there
was a very good juggler, a funny comedian
and some decent singers. The auditorium
filled up as the day went on until there
was quite a big crowd.

I was starting to think about leaving
when it was announced that the next act
was a magician.

'And here he is,' one of the judges
said. 'Michael Lewis!'

My jaw dropped as the reporter
walked out onto the stage. Michael Lewis
was a magician? Was that why he was

 183

so interested in me? He must have been pretty good if he'd nearly got to appear on television.

Michael bowed to the audience, pulled out a pack of playing cards and immediately dropped them on the stage. The crowd laughed. None more so than Bottley, who slapped his hands on his knees and rocked with laughter, shaking the row of seats.

Ah, I thought. Was this a comedy act?

Michael knelt and scrambled to collect the spilled cards. His hat fell off, releasing a dove, which immediately flew off into the lighting rig. He stared up in dismay. There was more laughter.

I frowned. His face suggested he wasn't enjoying the laughter. I didn't actually

think this was a comedy act. He was trying
to do proper magic. I mean, proper magic
tricks of course.

Michael was sweating and looked
nervous, and got a little more cross every
time someone laughed.

He shoved the messed-up cards back
in his pocket and pulled out a wand – or
at least he tried to, but it got stuck in his
pocket.

His trousers are too tight, I thought,
shaking my head. You need deep, open
pockets for ease of access. Magic 101.

Michael yanked at the wand. It came
loose with a jerk and slipped out of his
sweaty hand. It shot across the room
and hit Willow Holloughby in the eye.

She shrieked, clutched her face and fell backwards off her seat.

Then there was a long break in proceedings while someone from St John Ambulance came to check her over.

Bottley was crying with laughter throughout, but most people in the audience looked more concerned than amused. Everyone loved Willow Holloughby!

Michael looked sick as he waited to continue. I felt really bad for him. I knew what it was like when you dropped something or spilled something onstage.

'Sorry about that,' he said when we were ready to start again.

Willow now wore an eye patch and peered at him suspiciously.

'I just have one more trick to pull, and then I'm done. I'm confident you'll like this one though!' With that, Michael Lewis spun around quickly on the spot. I saw he was holding some kind of device with a button –

like a TV remote control maybe. He clicked it, and with a CRACK, a POP and a billowing cloud of smoke, he disappeared!

There was silence. Everyone looked stunned. He'd really pulled it off! After his terrible start, the crowd was totally behind him and he'd gone and nailed it! Bottley grunted, seemingly disappointed.

I started to clap, delighted that something had gone right for him. People joined in.

But then the smoke cleared. The applause faltered, then died away. Michael was still standing there, a pained expression on his face.

'F-F-F-Fire!' he cried.

'What?' one of the judges shouted.

'I'm on f-f-f-fire!' Michael screamed, then he ran straight toward the judges' table, trailing smoke and flames. Whatever the device had done hadn't just created smoke and a flash. It had set his trousers on fire!

'This is the best thing I've ever seen,' Bottley spluttered, leaning forward in his seat, rocking with laughter.

The crowd, after a moment's pause, also erupted in laughter, again assuming it was all part of the act. The judges were a little more wary, and they scattered as Michael crashed into their table. The hapless magician scrabbled desperately for a glass of water, but they all went tumbling as the table tipped over. Finally someone from the

 189

crew came running on with a fire extinguisher and blasted him all over with foam.

I just couldn't hold it in any longer.

I burst out laughing. Even though I genuinely felt sorry for poor Michael, the sight of him covered in foam, his trousers still smoking, while chaos erupted all around was far too funny for words.

I screamed with laughter until I got the hiccups, tears rolling down my face.

Just then Michael Lewis looked up and saw me there, helpless with mirth. His eyes flashed, his nostrils flared and his mouth twisted into a grimace. Then he got to his feet, turned around sharply and stalked offstage with as much dignity as he could muster.

I honestly wanted to stop laughing. But I couldn't. Neither could Bottley, or anyone else. Poor Michael the Magician left the room to the sound of hundreds of people screeching with laughter.

Who Is the Fairest
of Them All?

'Mirrors,' Gran said. 'That's how you do it.
Mirrors.'

I was through to the second round.
Or rather, **we** were through to the second
round. Me and Bottley. At some point I
would have to tell my parents I'd disobeyed
them, but I was trying not to think about

that. I needed to tell someone though, so I told Gran. And asked for her help with the trick. We had to make it even better.

'I don't understand,' I said. 'Won't the audience see the mirrors?'

'Not if you position them just right,' she said. 'You need to leave a little gap between them so your friend–'

'He's not my friend,' I said. 'I mean, not really . . .'

'So your beautiful assistant,' Gran corrected herself, 'can poke his arm through. They won't see that because you'll be standing in front of him. Of course.'

'Of course,' I said, frowning. 'I still can't quite get my head around how it works though.'

'I'll draw you a picture,' Gran said. She grabbed some paper and sketched out the trick.

'DOOSH! That is so clever,' I said. 'Gran, you're amazing. What would I do without you?'

'Let me give you some more advice,' she said. 'Two little words that will open doors for you your whole life.'

'What words?' I asked.

'Push and pull,' she said, then cackled at her own joke.

'But, Gran,' I said when she'd stopped laughing, 'where am I going to get these mirrors from?'

'I reckon we can find some down in the cellar,' she said.

We went down the stairs together. 'You know what?' Gran said. 'I'm thinking that maybe you should use a wire instead of getting your friend to lift you. There's less chance of it being seen.'

'I don't know,' I said. 'Bottley has been

 195

a big help to me so far. I don't want to leave him out now.'

'You don't have to leave him out,' Gran said. 'He can be the one who pulls you up on the wire. You'll need someone strong.'

'OK,' I said. 'That sounds like another great idea. You're so good at this!'

'I know,' she said.

'How come there aren't more female magicians?' I asked.

'There used to be loads,' Gran said. 'One day there might be a really famous female magician who could be the best in the world! You never know. Anything is possible!'

'Where have you been today?' Mum asked when I got home. She and Dad were sitting at the kitchen table. They looked like they'd been waiting for me.

'With the gang,' I said truthfully.

'Doing what?'

'Studying?' I said untruthfully.

'Rubbish,' Mum said. 'What were you doing?'

I hesitated. It's impossible to lie to Mum. I don't like lying at the best of times. I always feel really bad. I don't mind a bit of embellishment here and there; I don't always have to tell the **whole** truth. Leaving stuff out is different. But telling a bare-faced lie? That's not me.

Dad was just watching me, not saying

 197

anything. I could feel the waves of disappointment coming off him though. I was going to have to tell the truth. Sort of.

'I went to the first round of The Greatest Show on Earth,' I admitted. 'Stretch and Daisy were performing.'

'And what about you?' she said. 'Did you perform?'

Again, I hesitated.

That was enough for Mum.

'MAX!' she cried. Dad sighed.

'I couldn't help it!' I replied. 'Willow Holloughby was there, and she smiled at me. You can't say no when Willow Holloughby is smiling at you!'

'Your father told you to withdraw from the contest,' she said fiercely.

'But it's not fair,' I said, suddenly angry. 'This is my destiny. I have to follow my chi or else the universe will tip over!'

'Oh, for heaven's sake,' Dad snapped. 'Max, you **will** withdraw from the contest. You'll call them up right now and apologise, and then you'll go upstairs and get on with your homework.'

Suddenly I felt a wave of anger and my chest began to tingle. The magic surged through me, and before I could stop myself I blurted, 'Maybe you should forget we ever had this conversation. Maybe you should forget about my maths test result. Maybe you should be happy that I'm doing well in The Greatest Show on Earth.'

Everyone was silent for a few seconds.

 199

Mum and Dad blinked a couple of times, then Mum smiled. 'Where have you been today, Max?'

'Um . . . at The Greatest Show on Earth,' I said cautiously. 'I got through to the next round.'

'That's brilliant!' Mum said.

Dad grinned at me. 'Well done, Max,' he said. 'I'm proud of you.'

Lucky had heard the whole thing.

'Don't look at me like that,' I said when I got up to my room afterwards.

'Like what?' Lucky asked.

'Like you think I've just committed some terrible crime,' I said. The thing was, I

sort of agreed with Lucky. I'd just used magic on my parents to make them believe a lie.

'Are you sure you're doing the right thing?' Lucky asked.

'Look,' I said. 'Winning this competition could change everything. You know there's a cash prize, right? Ten thousand pounds. That sort of money would change everything for Mum and Dad. They could pay their bills, buy more stock for the stall.'

'Is that why you're doing this?' Lucky said. 'For the good of the family?'

'Well, why else?' I asked.

'Because you want to win the competition,' Lucky said. 'You want

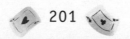

the fame and the attention. You want
the limousines and helicopters and the
paparazzi.'

'So, what's wrong with that?' I asked.

'Nothing,' Lucky said. 'As long as you're
honest about it. As long as you achieve all
that fair and square, without cheating.'

'I'm not cheating,' I said. 'There's a
reason I got these powers. It's destiny, it's
chi, it's everything!'

Lucky did a little doggie shrug. 'If you
say so,' he said.

But he was right. Of course he was
right.

What had I done?

13

In for a Penny

It was the morning of the second round, which was being held at the Festival Hall on the South Bank of the Thames. I looked at myself in the mirror, checking the top hat. Did I want it at a slight angle or straight, tilted forward, or back? People just don't understand how important angles and tilts

are when it comes to hats. I was wearing a purple shirt with a waistcoat. Lucky was watching me. He was cross because he wasn't allowed to come along to watch me.

'There are **other** dogs there,' Lucky pointed out.

'There is **one** other dog there,' I replied. 'Harry the Wonder Dog. Harry is one of the acts. He does tightrope walking and jumps through flaming hoops!'

'I could walk a tightrope,' Lucky said, scratching his ear with his hind leg. 'Nothing easier.'

'Yesterday in the park you fell in the duck pond,' I pointed out.

'Someone moved the duck pond,' Lucky grumbled. 'It didn't use to be there.'

'Sorry, Lucky,' I said. 'But you just can't come tonight.'

'Who's going to protect you?' he whined.

'Who would I need protection from?' I asked.

'Bottley the Bully of course!' Lucky said. 'I still haven't forgotten how he used to bash you and crash you and smash you. I have a bad feeling about this.'

'You're just being paranoid,' I said.

'I am paranoid,' Lucky agreed. 'But am I paranoid **enough**?'

I frowned into the mirror.

'What's wrong?' Lucky asked.

'I don't know,' I said. 'I have a strange feeling in my tummy.'

 205

'Your magic tingle?' he suggested.

'No, this is different,' I said. 'I feel sort of . . . sick . . .'

'Maybe you're feeling guilty about using magic on your parents.'

'Don't start that again,' I said.

'Actually, it sounds like you have a case of nerves,' Lucky said. He sat down on his haunches and started scratching behind his ear again.

'Nerves?' I said. 'That's ridiculous! I've never got nervous before a performance.'

'Well, maybe you've never given a performance that was this important to you,' Lucky said.

I looked at him and swallowed. He was

right. The words of Michael Lewis came back to me. Maybe you do only get one shot. And if you blow it? What then? What if my act goes the way his did?

All of a sudden I heard something in my head that Dad told me when he showed me how to do my first trick: 'Failing to prepare is preparing to fail!'

Only nine acts from each category had got through to this round. And only three in each category would go through to the semifinal, which would be held in Blackpool. I **really** wanted to go to Blackpool.

When I arrived, I was pleased to see that Mr Singh had turned up to support me.

 207

'You're going to smash it,' he said, clapping me on the back.

The competition in the Under-18s category included a twelve-year-old singer with the loudest voice I had ever heard, and a comedian called Jimmy Jokes. To be honest, I wasn't really worried about them. I reckoned Stretch would have had a better chance of beating me. Unfortunately for him, he'd been beaten by too much tea and too small a bladder.

I was more interested in the entrants in the other categories. In the Groups category there were three girls who rode unicycles while playing wind instruments. I saw one of them rolling around in the backstage area playing the theme tune from

'Jurassic Park' on the bassoon. There was
a girl pop band who sang in a beautiful
close harmony. Another entry in the Groups
category was a troupe of acrobats and
jugglers I was sure I'd seen on the South
Bank playing to crowds of tourists. They
were very professional and impressive.

I went to check out the Over-18s,
looking at the information sheet I'd been
given. There was a novelty act called Dr
Pickle and his partner, Harry the Wonder
Dog, there was a baritone singer named
Roland Benjamin, and then . . .

I blinked in surprise at the third name
on the sheet.

Mr Mysterio.

Another magician.

'Two magicians?' I asked the lady with the clipboard.

'There's no reason there can't be two magicians,' she said with a cheery grin. 'He's very good. And very **mysteeeerious**.'

'In what way?' I sniffed.

'He wears a mask,' she said. 'No one knows what he really looks like.'

'A mask, huh?' I said. And for the briefest second I thought about using my power of illusion to turn myself into a giant panther, or a tiny ant, or a psychic hellbeast from the planet Zorg. I had to take a deep breath. Whoever this Mr Mysterio was, I would defeat him fair and square. If I got through this round of course. But I'm nothing if not confident!

I paced around in the green room, going over my patter, trying out the jokes I was going to do. I needed to centre my chi and get the universe into some sort of balance. It was really hard to do, though, as my tummy was churning so much. Maybe I should have brought a pyramid!

Then I was interrupted by a voice.

'Hey, has anyone seen Max the Magnificent?'

I looked up and was met by the broad smile of Sophie. Behind her stood Daisy and Stretch.

'Oh, hi, guys,' I said, grinning. 'What are you doing here?'

'We came to help,' Daisy said. 'Since we're out of the competition now, we

 211

thought we'd get behind you and give our support. Team Max!'

I was really pleased. I had wondered if they might not want to come after our little squabble the last time.

'Yeah,' Sophie said. 'I have an idea for some audio-visual special effects, and maybe I could announce you. I know how to use all the equipment now.'

'And I thought you could ride onto the stage on the back of my bike,' Daisy said. 'You know, like a big entrance. I can juggle at the same time!'

'And I could come on first and do some somersaults across the stage,' Stretch said. 'To get everyone excited. I promise I've had a wee.'

'Oh,' I said. 'Well, that's very kind. But I think Bottley and I have it covered. I don't want to be changing the show at such a late stage, you see.'

Sophie blinked at me and cocked her head in surprise. 'You don't want our help?' she asked.

'It's not that,' I said. 'It's just that . . . well, to be honest, I'm trying to get my chi centred right now. It'll be great to know that you're in the audience watching though!'

'In the audience?' Stretch said, his face falling. 'Don't you want us on Team Max any more?'

'Um, well, you can be on Team Max,' I said. 'You know, supporting, from the

audience. I'm sure I can get Chloe to find you some great seats.'

'So you want us to sit in the audience, with everyone else, and cheer and clap and whistle?' Daisy asked.

'That'd be great, yeah!' I said.

'Fine,' Sophie said coldly. 'Come on guys, let's leave Max alone with his chi.'

The wire worked perfectly. Bottley and I had tested it out before the show – everyone got a few minutes to try out their act before the main event. There were only a few people in the auditorium at that point, but they all gasped as I went up. Clearly they couldn't see the wire. Gran had explained how to use lighting to make sure no one could see the thin cable.

In the show proper, it worked even better. Bottley lifted me at exactly the right time, in a smooth motion. I held my hands out to the sides to help me balance, but also to look like I was genuinely flying. I could have used my telekinesis to stop myself from swinging, but I was determined not to use my powers.

I got a huge round of applause, and I felt fairly confident I'd win my category – though the others were pretty good, I had to admit, especially the singer. She was tiny but she had a huge voice.

The very last act was Mr Mysterio. I watched from the wings with interest.

 215

I was curious to see what he'd come up with, and whether I could work out how he did his tricks. All magicians watch other magicians carefully – to see what they are up to and how good they are. But sometimes a bit of jealousy creeps in, if I'm being honest.

Mr Mysterio walked out onto the stage. He wore a mask that covered his entire face, and a simple dark robe with a hood. He looked spooky. My chest tingled a little, like I was nervous for someone else's trick. He stood still, facing the audience until the applause stopped and there was complete silence.

Then he disappeared.

And I don't mean in a flash, or in a puff of smoke. There was no noise, no distraction, no nothing. He just disappeared. I could see no mirrors, and I would definitely have been able to from where I was standding. It was the most astonishing thing I had ever seen. (Apart from perhaps when I'd made a massive

snake come out of the ground behind the science building at school.)

The audience **loved** it. They gasped in amazement, then clapped like crazy. I could even see Daisy, Stretch and Sophie standing up, cheering and stamping their feet. So much for Team Max.

Then Mr Mysterio reappeared. He bowed and left the stage. That was it. Just one trick. But what a trick it was! The simplicity of it had a certain appeal, I had to admit.

Bottley had also disappeared somewhere, so I went to join my friends while the judges deliberated.

'How did Mr Mysterio **do** that?' Stretch asked, his eyes wide.

'I don't know,' I said. 'But I'm going to find out.'

The three winners were announced.

'Freak Out!' the first judge cried.

'Max Magic!' the second judge yelled.

'And Mr Mysterio!' the third judge screamed.

Bottley thumped me on the back. I grinned up at him. We were through. We were going to Blackpool!

Devastating Discovery

The next day, after my shift on the stall, I went to see Gran to ask her how someone could just turn themselves invisible like that.

'At the risk of repeating myself,' Gran said, 'it's mirrors.'

'But I would have seen them,' I said. 'I know what to look for.'

'Oh, expert now, are we?' she said, raising an eyebrow.

'There were no mirrors, Gran,' I said. I was going to tell her about the tingle I'd felt just before Mr Mysterio disappeared.

'What are you suggesting?' she said. 'That he used . . . **real** magic?' She raised an eyebrow.

I shrugged. 'Do you believe in real magic, Gran?'

It wasn't the first time I'd asked her the question.

'I believe in whatever the punters will pay to see,' she said.

'That's not answering the question,' I said.

'Changing the subject,' she said, 'but

 221

your friend was in here again the other
day.'

'Which friend?' I asked.

'Your reporter friend,' she said. My
blood ran cold and I shot a glance at
Lucky, who looked back at me and nodded.

'What did he want?' I asked.

'Nosing about, he was,' Gran said. She
took a sip of her tea. Gran liked it very
hot. 'I left him alone while I went to serve
another customer, and next thing I knew,
he'd gone. Then I saw him later, coming
out of the back room. I asked him what
he thought he was doing in there, and
he didn't answer. He just looked at me
like he'd seen a ghost. White as a sheet,
he was. Then he ran out the door.' Gran

looked at me closely. 'You've gone white as a sheet too. Are you all right?'

I swallowed. The room swam and I thought I was going to faint. Michael Lewis had been in Gran's back room? But in Gran's back room was the door to the cellar.

Where the chest was.

'I think he might have pinched a candlestick,' Gran said, peering about the gloomy shop. She turned on some more lights. 'Could have sworn I had a nice silver candlestick just next to that signed photo of Harry Houdini.'

'I don't think he was here for candlesticks,' I muttered.

'What's that?' she asked, turning.

223

'Do you mind if I go and take a look in the cellar?' I asked.

Gran shook her head. 'Course not.'

Lucky at my heels, I went down the narrow steps, hoping my fears would not be realised, but when I got to the bottom and turned on the light, my heart sank. Arthur Andrews's chest sat there, the lid wide open. I knew I'd shut it last time I'd been here. Michael must have opened the chest. And he'd seen something that had terrified him – or something that had shocked him at least.

I turned on Lucky. 'Why didn't you stop him?' I asked. 'Or at least bark to get Gran's attention?'

Lucky looked guilty. 'I might have been asleep,' he said.

'Asleep?!'

'We elderly dogs need at least fourteen hours' sleep a day,' he said defensively. 'I have to recharge the batteries, so I have enough juice to defend you when you're around.'

'Well, thanks for nothing,' I said.

I thought furiously. Bottley **must** have overheard me talking to Sophie about the chest. I had seen him talking to Michael backstage at the town hall. Bottley must have told him about the chest. Now he'd found it and knew its secrets.

I'd been found out. By a reporter. I'd never be allowed to compete in The Greatest Show on Earth. I'd never get to go on television with Willow Holloughby

and win £10,000. No one would ever take me seriously as a magician. The press wouldn't leave me alone.

I'd miss my shot.

I sank to the floor, my heart pounding.

Everything had gone wrong.

I didn't sleep a wink that night. Mum kept asking me what was up, but I just told her I had a tummy ache. This is the problem when you have a big secret. You can't tell the people closest to you. The people you need. The people who can help.

I wondered if I should tell her. After all, the truth was about to come out anyway, wasn't it? Underneath it all was the awful feeling I'd been trying to block out from my mind. The feeling of guilt about lying to my parents. Using my mind-control powers on them. And for what? I was going to have to pull out of the competition anyway. Was this fate? Destiny? Chi? I'd done a bad thing and the universe was going to make sure I was punished.

I'd sent a message to the Team Max group chat on my phone, to see if anyone was around to chat, but no one replied. They were all cross with me. They thought I'd left them behind.

I couldn't talk to my 'new friend' Bottley either. He had told Michael Lewis about my powers. Sophie, Stretch and Daisy had been right. As had Lucky. I shouldn't have

 227

trusted Bottley. The only person I had to talk to about it was Lucky, and he wasn't even a person.

'He might not reveal your secret, Max,' Lucky said as I stroked his back. 'You didn't want to tell anyone about your powers – maybe he will feel the same way.'

'I told my friends,' I said. 'Before I betrayed them.'

'You haven't betrayed them,' Lucky said. 'They're just a little cross with you, just like I was when you didn't take me to the show. I forgave you. You'll see them tomorrow at school and sort everything out.'

I felt a bit better after that. Good old Lucky.

'Anyway,' he said, 'maybe we should try to get some sleep.'

'You need more sleep?' I asked, incredulous. But he was already snoring.

I raced downstairs first thing in the morning and snatched the 'East End Express' off the table just as Dad was reaching out for it.

'Oi,' he said.

I quickly scanned the front page, sure that there would be a big splash about me and my amazing powers.

Criminal Youths Target Nice People read the headline.

I looked at page 2, page 3, page 4.

Nothing in there involving me except on
page 6, where there was a short story about
a possible sighting of a grizzly bear in the
city. Nothing naming me or any mention
of magic. My heart lifted slightly. Maybe
Lucky had been right.

'Looking for something in particular?'
Dad asked.

'Just checking the, er, FTSE 5000 exchange,' I lied.

'Oh, you been investing?'

'You have to, er . . . postulate to, um . . . aggravate,' I said, tapping the side of my nose.

Dad looked confused and I took the opportunity to scarper. I wanted to get to school early and see Sophie, Stretch and Daisy. I was anxious to tell them what Bottley had done, as well as apologise to them for ever thinking he could replace them.

But my friends weren't the first people I saw at school. It was Bottley. He loomed out from behind a classroom, blocking out the sun. I glared at him, waiting for him

231

to try and deny what he'd done.

'Hi, Max,' he said brightly. 'Hey, I'm really excited about us going to Blackpool. I had some ideas for the show . . .'

He tailed off. 'What's wrong?'

'Have you been talking to Michael Lewis?' I asked. I was really cross. I didn't care how big Bottley was, or that he could have driven me into the ground like a tent peg. In fact, I felt like I was crackling with power. I hadn't used my powers for so long, they were pent up inside me and I was just itching for an excuse to blast him into the football goal some six metres away.

I'd done it before.

'Who's Michael Lewis?' he asked.

'The reporter,' I said. 'Don't try and wiggle out of this! I saw you talking to him at the audition.'

He looked confused. Then his face brightened. 'Oh, yeah, I talked to him. But he just asked me if I knew you. He wanted to interview you for his paper. I didn't think you'd mind. You always like the attention. Did I do something wrong?'

I narrowed my eyes and watched him carefully. If he was lying, he was hiding it very well.

'You didn't talk to him about . . . my gran's shop?'

He frowned in confusion. 'What about your gran's shop?'

'Well, maybe I made a mistake,' I said.

'Maybe I . . . misjudged you.'

He shrugged. 'It's understandable,' he said. 'You and I do have history after all.'

'I'm sorry,' I said.

Suddenly I felt very emotional. I hadn't slept and I felt like I had no friends. My lip wobbled a bit and Bottley stepped forward and gave me a great big bear hug. He squeezed too hard, and he smelled a bit like worms and fish, but I appreciated the hug nonetheless. I stepped back and said, 'Thank you.'

'It's fine,' he said. Then I looked up and saw Sophie, Stretch and Daisy watching me. Sophie raised an eyebrow, then the three of them turned and walked away.

For a moment I was going to run after

them, explain, apologise. But then Bottley spoke. 'Anyway, can I tell you about my ideas for the trick?'

I looked back at him and grinned. 'Sure, George,' I said. 'That would be **unbelievable**.'

15

Blackpool Bombshell

'I can't believe you're not coming to Blackpool,' I said to Gran.

'Well, I'm not getting any younger,' she said. 'And I don't like to travel far with these hips. Anyway, I've been to Blackpool more times than you've eaten a brownie.'

'It's still a shame,' I said. 'You're the

one who's been most supportive of me. Dad thinks I'm wasting my time.'

'He just wants what's best for you,' Gran said.

I decided to change the subject. I still felt bad about using my mind control on my parents. I didn't want to be reminded of it.

'What advice can you give me about Blackpool?' I asked.

'They like a bit of physical comedy,' she said. 'When in doubt, drop your trousers.'

'We're going to Blackpool!' Susie cried as the train pulled out of Euston Station. I think she was the most excited out of all of us, and we were all excited, except Dad,

who was annoyed about having to close
the stall for a couple of days. He was also
worried about the cost of the trip. But Mum
had insisted we all go together.

'We haven't had a holiday in years,'
she'd said. Mum was the only one of us
who'd been to Blackpool before – on a hen
weekend sometime in the late nineties, and
she couldn't remember much about that.

'I remember walking into the first pub,'
she said. 'And after that it's all a bit of a
blur.'

Vinny was hoping to squeeze in a trip
to Manchester to see his beloved West Ham
play Manchester City, and Chris was excited
about the illuminations.

'It's an engineering marvel!' he said

excitedly. 'They started in 1879. It's this big display of lights that stretches for six miles and has over one million bulbs.'

'Glad we're not paying that electric bill,' Dad said. He sighed. 'Shame your gran isn't here. She played Blackpool many times back in the day, with Grandpa. She used to talk about it a lot.'

The organisers of The Greatest Show on Earth had arranged a hotel for us. Though it was called the Grand, it wasn't exactly the Greatest Hotel on Earth. But it overlooked the sea, and from my window I could see the front and the sandy beach beyond it, through the rain. At night we'd be able to look out and see the illuminations.

 239

'Look at those gulls,' Lucky said. 'They look like they need chasing.'

'They're massive,' I pointed out. 'They'd probably carry you away.'

We had a few hours to kill before the rehearsals for the show, then the show itself was starting at 7 p.m. So we went for a walk along the front. Although this show wasn't on television, there had been quite a bit of interest on social media, and it was exciting to see posters for the show around the town. My name was on there! Quite near the bottom. But it was there! My name in lights. Sort of.

'I think I remember that club,' Mum said, staring at a dilapidated building. 'It looked a bit more glamorous in the nineties.'

'Everything did,' Dad said. Mum narrowed her eyes at him.

Susie looked slightly disappointed by Blackpool, but Mum assured her that the town only really came to life when it got dark. 'This town is going to shine tonight,' she said, and gave me a wink.

Lucky loved it, of course. He hoovered
up the chips and battered sausages that
littered the pavement. He chased the gulls,
then raced across the beach and splashed
in the sea. Since I'd got my powers and
discovered I could talk to him, sometimes
it seemed like Lucky was more person than
dog. But he was definitely in Dog Mode
here in Blackpool. As I watched him charge
through a family trying to have a peaceful
picnic on the beach, scattering their
sandwiches, I thought maybe we could all
learn a lesson from Lucky. Maybe we should
all move into Dog Mode from time to time
and cast our worries aside.

My phone pinged. I checked it and saw
three messages.

Sophie: Good luck tonight x

Daisy: You're going to smash it!

Stretch: Wish I was there to watch.
See you on Monday, Max Magic!

Then another message arrived. From
Sophie.

Sophie: BTW I have another page
of the diary. VV interesting. Let's
talk later! x

 243

So when we arrived at the Showtime Ballroom later that day, I felt much happier. I'd left Michael Lewis behind in London and he seemed to have gone quiet. I was here in Blackpool, with my family, doing what I loved most. My dad was doing his best to be supportive, my friends were still my friends, and my dog was still my dog. Everything was going to be OK.

The Showtime Ballroom, like most of Blackpool, looked a bit shabby on the outside. But when I went in, it was revealed to be a spectacular grand old theatre.

'It's beautiful,' Susie said.

'It's glorious,' Mum said.

'It's magic,' Dad said, a huge grin on his face.

One of the organisers came up to us. This one also had a clipboard and a ponytail, but I think it was a different girl with a different clipboard and ponytail because this one had a northern accent.

'Let me guess,' she said with a grin. 'Max Magic, right?'

'What gave it away?' I asked, taking off my top hat and bowing. The rest of the family was directed to a room where they could have a cup of tea while I went through to the backstage area with the other acts.

I caught up with Bottley in the green room. He'd been fishing with his dad during the day and smelled quite strongly

 245

of mackerel, but it was good to see his friendly face.

Mr Singh showed up as well.

'I couldn't miss this,' he said. 'I'll be taking photos and cheering you on from the crowd.'

We watched the other acts stretching and rehearsing their lines while we waited for our turn to practise, then ran through the trick one more time. Everything went just fine. Then it was just a matter of waiting. I watched the other acts; they were very good, especially a dance troupe from Scotland called Inclusivity. Interestingly, Mr Mysterio didn't turn up for his rehearsal.

'He emailed to say he didn't need it,' the clipboard lady said, shrugging.

Despite my earlier good mood, my nerves grew again as we waited, especially when we could hear the audience coming in. I took myself off to find a quiet spot to balance my chi again. I've never met anyone who can describe what the actual feelings of nerves are, but I don't think there is a single person in the world who hasn't experienced it.

And then, before I knew it, it was my turn. Fox Blackshaw introduced me and there was a huge roar from the audience. I don't know how many people were there watching, but it sounded like a million. I took a deep breath. Bottley clapped me on the shoulder and I walked out onto the stage to begin my patter.

'There's this girl at school I like,' I said, 'but when I told her I was a magician, she disappeared.'

The roar when we completed the levitation trick was like nothing I'd ever experienced before. I'd performed in front of crowds before, sure. On the stall, at school, even at the earlier round in London. But this was something else. When Bottley hauled me up, the crowd just went wild. Whoever was handling the spotlight was amazing – they followed me up into the air, my sparkly waistcoat dazzling in the bright lights.

The feeling was better than Christmas, better than my birthday, better than any time when I'd used my magical powers and felt the thrill run through me.

This was what I wanted to do. This was what I wanted to be. Soaring high above a clapping, cheering crowd. Everyone watching me. Everyone thinking, How did he do **that**?!

Finally I was Max the Magnificent.

 249

Later on, still buzzing, I sat in the wings
to watch Mr Mysterio do his trick. Lucky
was beside me. Once the magician had
finished, there would be interviews with the
local papers and a photographer was going
to take some pictures for social media.
Then, once the judges had totted up the
points, the winners of each round would
be announced – just three performers who
would go head to head in the grand finale
at the Globe.

'I wonder who he is,' I said. 'It's
supposed to be amateurs in this talent
show. But he's so good I wonder if he's
one of the big names. Like the Great

Mancini, or Simon the Sorceror or that guy who presents that game show . . . what's his name?'

'I don't remember,' Lucky said.

As Mr Mysterio came past, he stopped and looked at me.

Suddenly, without thinking, without even **trying**, I was reading his mind.

'You,' he thought, 'Max Magic, the boy with the chest.'

And suddenly I knew who was behind the mask. I gasped and stepped back.

'What is it, Max?' Lucky said. 'What's wrong? Should I bite him?'

But before I could respond, Mr Mysterio was gone.

'I know who Mr Mysterio is,' I said.

 251

'Who?!'

'The reporter,' I said. 'Mr Mysterio is Michael Lewis!'

My family and Mr Singh had been allowed to join me in the green room while the judges made their deliberations. As I entered, they came rushing up to congratulate me. But I was too preoccupied by Michael Lewis to really appreciate them. What did this mean? How had this local newspaper reporter gone from being the worst magician on Earth to being able to disappear?

I thought I knew the answer, but I wasn't sure.

'Nervous about the result, Max?' Mum said, seeing my face. 'You shouldn't be. You were the best one up there.'

'And if the magic thing doesn't work out,' Vinny said, 'you and Bottley can always go into business together cleaning windows.'

'What?'

'Well, he can haul you up on that cable thing and you can do the wiping.'

'Thanks, Vince,' I said. 'I'll bear it in mind.'

'I think I can design a portable version of the block and tackle,' Chris said thoughtfully. 'You could hook it to the top of a skyscraper and up you go. No reason you couldn't go up twenty floors and stay

 253

there for as long as Bottley's arms hold
out.'

'Good trade, window cleaning,' Dad
said. 'The world is full of windows – and
dirt.'

'Sam!' Mum snapped.

'What? I'm just saying that there's
money in window cleaning–'

'Look' I said. 'I know you're trying
to help. At least I think you're trying to
help. But I don't want to be a window
cleaner. And much as I appreciate George
Bottley having turned a corner, I'm not
sure I trust him to haul me sixty metres
in the air so I can wipe a squeegee across
the office window of some city banker.'

'Max is going to win The Greatest Show

on Earth,' Susie said, glaring at the more disloyal members of my family.

While we'd been having this argument, Fox Blackshaw had come onstage and tapped on the microphone, startling us. We scurried out into the auditorium and took up our reserved seats near the front.

'Look at his tight trousers,' Mum said. 'I'm suddenly having flashbacks to the hen do.'

I looked around, wondering if Mr Mysterio was here. What exactly was he planning?

'And now it's time to reveal the winners of each category,' Fox began. 'The three acts who will get to perform in front of the nation on Saturday . . .'

'Come on . . .' I muttered, peering towards the entrance to see if Mr Mysterio had arrived. Maybe he would be knocked out of the competition here, I thought.

'He's just building up tension,' Susie whispered. 'They always do this.'

'A performance that will be televised,

reaching millions of viewers!' Fox went on. 'And the winner on the night will receive a cash prize of £10,000!' There was a big round of applause at this, especially from Dad.

Fox paused until there was quiet. 'Here are the names,' he said in a hushed tone. 'In no particular order . . .'

Then there was a long pause. The lights went down, leaving just one spotlight. The music played low and tense, the thumping matching the rhythm of my heart.

'Inclusivity!'

The audience went wild and the spotlight waved all over the place. It settled on the dancers at the far side of the auditorium. They were leaping about, hugging each other and doing back flips. Then, as the applause faded and the crowd hushed, the lights went down again and the spotlight was again trained on Fox.

'The second act to go through is . . .'

This time, the pause was even longer.

'Mr Mysterio!' Fox yelled. There were more cheers, though not as loud as for Inclusivity. Mr Mysterio didn't seem to have brought any friends and family. The spotlight weaved around in the crowd, trying to find him. I swallowed. Where had he gone? Back to London? Back to Gran's shop? Or was he waiting for me outside?

'Never mind, Max,' Dad said. 'You did your best.'

'There's still one place available,' Mum pointed out, jabbing Dad in the ribs.

'They're not going to have two magicians in the final, are they?' Dad said.

'They'll pick the comedian, or the girl with the wobbly voice.'

'Not the wobbly-voice girl,' Vinny groaned. 'She was so **loud**.'

'Mr Mysterio is unfortunately not able to be here right now,' Fox said apologetically. 'He has disappeared.'

The crowd laughed. I took a deep breath, trying to balance my chi.

'And so the last act to go through to the final next week,' Fox said when things had calmed down, 'is . . .'

The lights went down again. The music swelled. The audience hushed. I held my breath. It seemed the whole room was holding its breath.

All except Fox. He took a deep lungful

of air, then leaned in to the microphone.

'Max Magic!' he yelled.

I called Team Max from the hotel room
after the performance. It felt good
to see them all, and they were all
absolutely chuffed for me when they
heard I was through to the final. To
be honest, I didn't feel chuffed. I felt
worried about what Michael Lewis had
planned. And I felt guilty. All I could
think of was how I'd used my mind
control on my parents. How I'd lied.
How I'd cheated. I'd been trying not to
think about it. Trying to excuse my own
behaviour in a hundred different ways:

it was only a little lie . . . We needed the money . . . This was a wake-up call for me . . . I'd work harder at school from now on . . .

But none of that stopped me feeling guilty. Not deep down. So I was quick to move on from listening to my friends' words of support. I honestly needed the distraction.

'So, tell us what you discovered in Arthur's diary!' I said.

'OK!' Sophie said, looking excited. She opened her notebook and began to read.

Something extraordinary happened today. I can hardly write. My hand is shaking so much. I needed a stiff brandy just to

 261

settle myself enough to sit at my writing desk.

This morning the locksmith arrived. The hotel concierge had told me he was the best in the city, and it took him a matter of minutes to unlock the chest. As the catch clicked, the man took hold of the lid to open the chest, but I cried out a sharp warning not to do so. He looked surprised, but I paid him handsomely and ushered him out of the room.

I locked the door behind him, then turned to the chest. My heart was pounding. I stepped forward, took hold of the lid, and opened it.

I had not expected what was to come. There was a flash and a bang, and I

found myself flung across the room.
When I recovered my senses I . . .

Sophie stopped reading.

'I what?' Daisy asked. 'Keep going.'

'I couldn't make out the rest,' Sophie
said. 'The page was too damaged.'

'Sophie!' I cried. 'You can't leave us
hanging like this!'

'You're welcome to have a try,' Sophie
said.

'I'm sorry,' I said. 'You've done a
great job. Do you think there might be
more pages you can read?'

'I think so,' Sophie said. 'But it's
taking time. And I need to study.
Remember studying, Max?'

'OK, OK, sorry,' I said. 'Let us know if and when you manage to figure out any other passages.'

'I will.'

'And, Sophie,' I said. 'Thank you.'

16

No Show

'So you're not coming to the final?' I asked
Gran, disbelieving.

She shook her head. 'Sorry, Max,
my hips just aren't up to it, I'm afraid.
Besides, someone needs to look after Lucky.
And I can watch on the telly.'

I sat down and sighed. It was only a

couple of days before the final. This last week had passed slower than any week in history. I was just desperate for it to be over. I hadn't been sleeping well, what with worrying about Michael Lewis, feeling guilt over my deception and outright panic about the exams that were coming up soon. I'd really hoped Gran might make it. Suddenly everything felt a bit much. Lucky put his head on my knee and I scratched his ears.

'What's troubling you, Max?' Gran asked.

'I'm sad that you can't make it to the show,' I said.

'That's not all, is it?' Gran said. She handed me the plate of brownies. 'I know you. And something has been bothering you for a couple of weeks now.'

I looked at her. How did she know? There was no point hiding it any more, and I really wanted to talk to someone about how I'd been feeling. But I couldn't tell her the **whole** truth. I had to be careful.

'I failed a maths test,' I said. 'And I . . . sort of lied to Mum and Dad about it.'

'Why did you lie?' Gran asked.

'Because I know that if they knew I'd done really badly, they'd make me pull out of The Greatest Show on Earth.'

'What will they do if they find out you've lied to them?' Gran asked.

'They'll probably skin me alive,' I said.
'Then roast me over a fire. Then send me
to bed without any tea.'

'You lied to them because you were
desperate to be in the show?'

'Yes.'

'Because you're good at magic. Because
this is your thing?'

I nodded. 'Yes,' I repeated.

'Then tell them that,' Gran said. 'Make
them understand how you **feel**. Your
parents are not bad people. They want
you to do well. They understand more
than anyone that we have to make difficult
choices sometimes. But this one isn't
difficult. It's not even close. You have
to tell them the truth.'

'And if they tell me I can't compete in the final?' I asked.

'Then you accept it and move on. There'll be other competitions,' Gran said.

'But what if this is my one shot?' I asked.

'There's always another shot,' Gran said.

I was in a reflective mood as Lucky and I left Gran's shop on the way home. London felt very autumnal. Rain was in the air, and the streetlights were already on.

'I can't believe no dogs are allowed,' Lucky muttered.

'I told you,' I said. 'I got an email

 269

saying no pets would be allowed at the final, apart from performers and guide dogs.'

'I could be a guide dog!' Lucky said.

'You fell down a drain yesterday,' I reminded him.

'Because I was distracted by a doughnut!' he said. 'So, are you going to tell them?' He paused. 'Your parents.'

'Yes,' I said.

'When?'

'What do you mean?'

'Are you going to tell them now? Or **after** the final of The Greatest Show on Earth?'

'Oh great, so now you're reading my mind too?' I asked.

'You're pretty transparent,' Lucky said.

I turned into an alley – a shortcut through to Bishopsgate.

'Why are we going this way?'

'It's a shortcut,' I said.

'The last time we went down this street, we were attacked by Bottley the Bully,' Lucky pointed out. 'Let's go the long way around.'

The rain fell harder. 'Look,' I said, 'Bottley isn't stalking me any more. There's nothing to worry about. Besides, have you forgotten I have magic powers?'

Lucky shook his head but followed me into the dark alley.

We'd only gone a few steps when I heard footsteps behind me.

I stopped and turned around, but there was nobody there.

Lucky sniffed. 'I can smell someone.'

'There's no one there,' I said. 'Come on.' We carried on walking. Again, I heard footsteps behind. Again, Lucky sniffed the air.

'Did you hear that?' I asked.

'Did you smell that?' Lucky said.

But there was still nothing there. I could see all the way to the end of the alley, where the warm, welcoming glow of a streetlight made me wish I'd taken Lucky's advice.

I turned and went to take another step.

Then someone appeared before us as if from nowhere.

It was Mr Mysterio.

Lucky growled.

'Hello, Mr Lewis,' I said.

Michael Lewis laughed. He took off his mask. 'I should have known you'd figure out my real identity,' he said. 'You're a smart kid. And polite.'

'That reminds me,' I said. 'I want to say sorry. About laughing when your trick went wrong at the town hall.'

He nodded. 'Thank you. Maybe I was right about you after all.'

I had no idea what he meant.

'I know you opened the chest,' I said cautiously. 'I know you gained the power of invisibility.'

'Not just invisibility,' Michael said.

 273

'Maybe I'll show you my other power later.'

'What do you want?' I asked.

'The same things everyone wants,' Michael said. 'Power, wealth, success. I intend to win The Greatest Show on Earth, then embark on a global tour, showing off my powers. I will be the greatest magician this world has ever seen. No one will ever laugh at me again.'

I shook my head. 'When I first gained my powers, I used them for the wrong reasons and it taught me a lesson. We shouldn't use our powers to benefit ourselves.' I said.

'Nonsense,' Michael spat. 'We've been given these powers for a reason, Max. Don't you see? We can become great.'

'We?' I narrowed my eyes at him.

'Yes, Max. That is what I'm talking about. I see something in you. And I think the chest saw the same thing.' He was earnest and urgent. 'You and I are the same, Max.'

I shook my head. 'We're not the same.'

'I'm offering you the chance to join me,' he said. 'To be my partner. Max the Magnificent and Michael the Marvellous. Together with the chest in your gran's shop, we could rule more than the stage. We could rule the world!'

'You're crazy,' I said. 'And you'd better stay away from my gran!'

'Join me, Max!' he cried.

I shook my head again. 'I won't misuse

my powers for cheap tricks on the stage,' I said. 'And you shouldn't either.'

He took a step forward. Lucky growled again.

'I could have used my powers to defeat you, and stop you from competing in the contest,' he said in a low voice. 'But I didn't. I thought I would extend the hand of friendship. I advise you to take it, Max.'

'Do you think you're stronger than me?' I asked.

Suddenly Michael whipped up a hand and shot a hot, bright ball of fire right past my head. I spun to watch it go, and saw it slam into a large recycling bin a few metres away. The bin went up in a big ball of flame. Lucky yelped in alarm. I turned back

to Michael, who was laughing at me.

'How come **he** gets fireballs?' Lucky
said.

I remembered the heady feeling of
power I had when I misused **my** magic. I
could tell Michael Lewis wasn't going to
see reason. He was drunk with power. And
unfortunately **he** didn't have three good
friends and a loyal dog to stop him from
going too far.

'The answer is no,' I said.

His face turned dark. 'So be it,' he
said. 'I won't give you another chance.
Withdraw from the competition tonight
and I'll leave you and your precious gran
alone.'

And with that he was gone. I heard

a fire alarm ringing and the shouting of people coming to investigate the flames.

'Come on, Lucky,' I said, shaking all over. 'Let's get home.'

'OK,' Lucky said. 'Oh, and Max?'

'Yeah?'

'Let's not go down this alley ever again.'

I didn't tell Mum and Dad everything, obviously. That would have been too much. There were some secrets I wasn't ready to share – and they weren't ready to hear.

I told them pretty much the same story I'd told Gran. That I'd failed my maths test. And that I had covered it up. We sat at the dining-room table while my brothers

and sister were in the sitting room, laughing at some reality TV show.

'Why didn't you tell us?' Mum said. She was doing most of the talking. Dad was just sitting there, not looking at me. His face was grim.

'I thought you'd stop me entering The Greatest Show on Earth,' I said.

'Too right,' Dad said.

For half a second I thought about answering back. But then I remembered what Michael Lewis had said. What was the point? If I was to bring the universe back into balance, I had to pull out of the competition.

'I'll phone Mr Singh tomorrow and pull out of the competition,' I said.

'Tonight,' Dad said.

'Sam,' Mum said, placing a hand on his wrist, 'Max has done the right thing in owning up to this.'

'A bit late,' Dad muttered. He looked at me finally. 'Call your teacher.'

Mr Singh took it really well, considering. I think he wanted to scream though.

'The final is tomorrow,' he said. 'The organisers are going to be furious. Willow Holloughby is going to hate me. Do you know what it's like to be hated by Willow Holloughby?!'

'I'm sorry,' I said.

'Your name is on all the posters, and on

the TV ad that's going out tonight. It's too late to change.'

'They'll just have to get the runner-up to perform in my place. It was Jimmy Jokes. He is fantastic.'

'He is?' Mr Singh replied.

'Of course! His act is an absolute tour de force. It would be a crime for his brilliance to be withheld from the public.'

Mr Singh sighed. 'OK, Max. I know you wouldn't be doing this if it wasn't absolutely necessary.'

'Thanks, Mr Singh.'

I called my friends later on to give them the news. They were all very sympathetic.

I could tell Sophie wanted to say 'I told you so' about me not studying, but she kept quiet.

'Would it help take your mind off it,' she said, 'if I told you I've managed to translate another page of the diary?'

'Yes!' I said. 'That would help a lot.'

'So, there's good news and bad news,' Sophie went on.

'What's the good news?' Daisy asked. Daisy always liked to hear good news first. She says that once you've heard good news, it usually doesn't matter what the bad news is. I like it the other way around. If I'm hearing bad news, I like to know there's good news still to come. Like eating your carrots before your chips.

 283

'The good news is that you're going to find this extract very interesting,' she said.

'And the bad news?'

'I've looked through the rest of the diary and the water damage is just too bad for me to read any more.' She looked disappointed.

'Let's hear it then,' I said.

Sophie opened her Business Book and began to read.

I found my new power extremely useful today. I was beset by ruffians in a quiet back street who wanted my wallet – and possibly my life. Instead, they found themselves staring up at me in fear and astonishment as I levitated high above them, safely out of reach.

'Levitation!' I cried. 'The chest gave Arthur the power of levitation!'

'Pretty cool, huh?' Sophie grinned.

'Yeah, that's amazing,' Daisy agreed.

'Awesome!' Stretch said. 'What's levitation?'

'The ability to raise yourself off the ground without assistance,' I said. 'Like my stage trick but without Bottley.'

'There's more,' Sophie said. I nodded and she began to read again.

The thugs turned and ran, one of them gabbling as he went. He was saying the same word over and over again: djinn.

'My gran drinks gin,' Stretch said.

'Not gin, d-j-i-n-n,' Sophie said. 'It's another name for a genie. I looked it up. Djinn were spirits with magical powers. But hold on, there's a bit more.' She read from the paper again.

I have been mulling over his cries ever since.

Has that street thug provided me with the answer to the puzzle? Is this the nature of the power within the chest? Could it be a djinn?

One thing is for sure. There is great danger in the powers granted by the chest. They are a boon, but also a deadly trap. A man could lose his soul if he misuses the gifts the chest grants.

Sophie stopped. 'That's all there is.'

'Well, that explains a few things,' I said thoughtfully.

'Surely you don't believe there is actually a djinn in the chest?' Sophie rolled her eyes.

'Arthur Andrews seems to think that,' I replied. 'That's what he meant in the first extract, when he asked **who** might be inside. He believed there was a spirit inside the chest. And I agree when he says the powers should not be misused. Remember when I went OTT and nearly choked Bottley with the giant worm?'

'Come off it though! A genie?' Sophie shook her head. 'Like Aladdin? Three wishes and all that?'

'If you'd asked me a month ago, I would have said there's no such thing as djinns,' I said. 'But then I opened the chest. And now I'm willing to believe pretty much anything.'

The next morning I woke feeling rotten. The event I'd been looking forward to for months had finally arrived, and I wasn't going to be there. Mr Singh had said I could still go along and watch.

But I couldn't bear to do that. To watch Michael Lewis take the prize. Besides, he'd basically told me he was going to burn me to a crisp if I showed up. It was time to put it all behind me. In fact, maybe it was time to get up and open a maths book.

I lay in bed, not moving.

'Are we getting up?' Lucky asked. He was lying at my feet.

'Nope,' I said.

'I'm hungry,' he said.

'You're always hungry,' I said.

'I'm **really** hungry,' he went on.

I was about to tell him to shut up when the door opened and someone came in.

'Gran?'

'Aren't you supposed to be at the Globe?' she said.

'I pulled out,' I said. 'I told Mum and Dad I'd lied to them, and they made me withdraw. It's kind of a relief, to be honest.'

'You can't withdraw,' Gran said. 'This is your big shot.'

'You said there are always more shots.'

'You don't want to listen to me,' Gran said. 'Phone them up and tell them you're performing after all.'

'I can't,' I said. 'It's too late. And Dad would kill me. I mean, Mum would kill me too. But Dad would kill me even more.'

'Don't worry about your mum and dad,' she said. 'I'll talk to them, smooth things over.'

I sat up. 'Are you serious?'

'Of course I'm serious,' she said. 'Now get up and have a wash. I'll sort out some breakfast. Then we're off to the Globe. You can come too, Lucky.'

'Dogs aren't allowed,' I said.

'Well, I'm in the mood for breaking rules today,' Gran said.

'Let me get this straight,' Mr Singh said. 'Now you want to re-enter the competition?'

'Yes.'

'What about Jimmy Jokes?'

'Terrible,' I said. 'Worst act I've ever seen.'

He sighed a long sigh. 'Fine. 'I'll give them a call now. But you'd better not change your mind again.'

'I won't,' I said. And I meant it. I knew Michael Lewis wasn't going to react well

 291

when he saw me arrive. But what could he do onstage, in front of all those people? And after that? Well, I had a plan forming in my mind . . .

Gran cooked me some breakfast, which I wolfed down.

My phone rang as I was mopping up the last of the runny egg yolk with my toast. It was Mr Singh.

'OK,' he said. 'They weren't happy, but they've agreed to let you back in.'

'Great!' I said.

'But you do need to be there in person to register at 9 a.m.,' he said.

'Fine,' I said. Then I looked at the clock. 8.39.

'Oh, **DOOSH**,' I said. I hung up. How

could I get to the Globe in twenty-one minutes? The Tube would take me forty minutes. Bus even longer. I could run, maybe.

Maybe.

Then it came to me. I groaned. But I knew there was no other way. I dialled a number on my phone.

'Daisy?'

'Just promise me you won't take any risks, OK?' I said.

'I never make promises I can't keep,' Daisy said. 'Now climb on.'

I got on the back of Daisy's bike and said a little silent prayer.

'All set?' Daisy asked.

'Hit it,' I said.

Daisy reached into her pocket and brought out a pair of aviator sunglasses. She flipped them open and put them on.

'Let's roll,' she said.

Then we were off.

I'd thought I could never be more terrified than the last time I was on Daisy's bike. But this was worse. Even Mr Mysterio shooting a fireball at me had been a picnic compared to the sheer terror of racing into oncoming traffic, car horns blaring, drivers shouting. Daisy took us up stairs, down narrow alleys, through flowerbeds and over tiny bridges. She went down an escalator and through a shopping mall, sending people scattering, before bursting out the back doors of a department store and over some railings onto the riverside walkway.

But the worst bit was when we went over Tower Bridge. The barriers came down just as we approached, and the bell started ringing to indicate that the bridge was lifting to allow a tall ship to pass through.

'We'll have to stop, Daisy,' I shouted. 'We can take London Bridge instead.'

'London Bridge is boring,' Daisy replied. 'Besides, there's no time.' She zipped around the barriers and pedalled like a demon, even though the bridge had started to rise.

'This a **bad idea**!' I wailed.

'I saw this in a film!' Daisy screamed. 'Hang on!'

 295

Then we were airborne. I felt sick.
It must only have been for a couple of
seconds – the bridge wasn't raised very
far – but my whole life flashed before my
eyes. To be fair, my life story was extremely
entertaining since I was the star, but it
wasn't what I wanted to watch right then.

We landed with a crunch, and the wind
was knocked out of me. Daisy raced on and
picked up speed down the slope on the other
side. A man in a uniform appeared at the
side of the road looking angry, waving his
fist. Daisy waved back.

'Keep your hands on the handlebars!' I
screamed.

We shot past him, skidding around the
barriers, and then we were down the steps

on the other side and whizzing along the South Bank.

'Don't worry. You're allowed to cycle here!' Daisy shouted at me.

'Like that would make a difference to you,' I muttered.

Five minutes later we skidded to a stop outside the Globe. The time was 8.57 a.m.

'You can let go now,' Daisy said. My hands were still digging into her shoulders as if I was an eagle clutching its prey. I released them with difficulty and got off the bike. She grinned at me.

'Th-thank you,' I said.

'What are you waiting for?' she cried. 'Go!'

The Worm Turns

I stood, the lights nearly blinding me. I was hot, I was nervous and I was alone. The applause died away.

When I'd arrived this morning Michael Lewis had seen me almost immediately. He'd given me a look of cold fury that made my blood curdle. I'd managed to avoid him during the day, as the acts split up and prepared for our performances. He hadn't turned up for his rehearsal again, which made me nervous. Was he off somewhere, causing trouble for Gran?

The day had been long, and full of things to worry about. Bottley turned up mid-morning and I remembered then that I'd completely forgotten to tell him I'd pulled out, then re-entered the competition. Oh well. No harm, no foul.

But now the moment was here. I took a deep breath. I took a deep breath and wished I had Mr Mysterio's power so I could become invisible, turn and run off the stage. This was it. This was my chance. My shot. And I wasn't at all sure I was

up to the challenge. But then I saw Gran in the audience, about six rows back. She had Lucky on her lap. And beside her sat Stretch, Daisy and Sophie. I grinned.

Then I saw someone else. In the front row.

It was Mr Singh. He gave me a wink and a thumbs up.

And there in front of Mr Singh sat the three judges: Fox Blackshaw, Shussy D and Willow Holloughby. She beamed at me, and I felt so much better. Part of me wondered if Willow Holloughby possessed a little magic of her own.

For the final, we had longer to do our turn. Fifteen minutes, if we wanted it. Fifteen minutes is longer than it sounds when you have a thousand people watching you. My plan was to do a few tricks, a few jokes, a bit of mind reading. Then the showstopper. The levitation trick.

I grinned. 'I know what you're thinking,' I said to the audience. 'Who is this kid, and why is he so handsome?'

That got a few titters.

'Some people think I'm too young to be a magician,' I said. 'And it's true that it takes years of practice and great discipline to become a magician. Do you know what a magician does first thing every morning – and I mean **every** morning?'

'No, what?' someone in the front row called. I winked at him. It was Mr Singh.

 301

He knew exactly what to say because we'd been through this before the show.

'They wake up.'

I squinted up at the lights. 'Those are bright,' I said. 'Speaking of lights . . . how many magicians does it take to change a lightbulb?'

'How many?' Mr Singh shouted.

I waggled my fingers mysteriously. 'That depends on what you want it changed into.'

More laughter.

The crowd was starting to relax, and so was I. Suddenly I was away. I sneezed and pulled a bright red handkerchief out of my pocket. It was attached to a second, and a third. Before long I'd pulled hundreds of the things out. I got myself in a tangle and

fell over. The crowd roared with laughter.
A bit of physical comedy, Gran would say.
And I didn't even need to drop my trousers.

I did my coin tricks, read a few minds
(without **actually** reading minds). I did my
tablecloth trick without spilling a drop.
Things were going well. I can do this, I
thought. I checked my watch. Time for the
main event. The showstopper. I backed up
against the mirrors and gave the signal to
Bottley. I felt him hook the wire onto the
harness at my back. I braced myself for the
lift, hoping he'd do it smoothly this time.
Everything had gone perfectly so far. I just
had to finish off, and I thought I had a
good chance of winning. Or at least of not
making a fool of myself.

I felt the hook pull against the harness.
I held my breath.

Then I was yanked into the air at terrific
speed. All the wind was knocked out of me.

I wanted to scream with the shock,
but I had no air in my lungs. What was
happening? The crowd seemed surprised.
Some people laughed, while others called
out in concern. It must have been clear
that this wasn't supposed to happen. I spun
and twisted in the air, unable to steady
myself. I looked down and saw Bottley.

He was looking back up at me, laughing.
He held up his finger in a hook shape.

'Like a little wriggly worm,' he said.
Then he turned and ran off into the wings,
leaving me helpless.

Just then I looked out, over the
audience, and saw the big double doors
open at the back of the Globe. My family
walked in. Vinny, Chris, Susie, Mum. And
Dad. They stopped and just stood there,
watching me dangling three metres above
the stage.

It felt like I was hanging there for an age. I expected the stage crew to come on and help me get down. I looked out into the wings, to see a few black-shirted crew desperately trying to untie the wire so they could release me. But Bottley must have secured it too well. They were going to have to cut it. But they'd need something pretty heavy-duty for that. This wasn't going to be quick. The crowd still seemed unsure how to react. I spun around slowly, the spotlights burning into me each time I swung around to face them, as if I was a bug under a microscope.

I couldn't believe Bottley had done this to me. I was so sure he'd changed. I had stood up for him when my friends were suspicious. Those acting classes he'd been taking had clearly paid off. He'd got me. Hook, line and sinker.

It was time to use my powers – not to cheat, but just to tip the universe back into balance. To restore my chi!

I pointed at the cable, where it was tethered to the bolt in the floor.

'Move back,' I called.

The crew looked up and hurriedly retreated. Maybe there'd been something in my voice. They could tell I was serious. I took a deep breath, I felt the power building in my chest, then I let it out.

The cable broke with a crack.

I fell to the stage, landing heavily then

 307

rolling forward, the way Stretch had shown me. I rolled over twice before ending up back on my feet. I bowed. The crowd cheered. I'm not sure what they thought was going on. But I was certainly putting on a show.

I looked out at the audience. What now? My big trick had been ruined. What did I have to offer the crowd? Instinctively I pushed my hand into a pocket and found something in there. I pulled it out.

It was the pack of cards. The Dragonscales. I looked out into the crowd and saw my dad watching me carefully.

He nodded. And smiled.

I shuffled the pack and looked down at Mr Singh.

'You, sir,' I said. 'Pick a card. Any card.'

18

Showstopper

'In third place . . .'

The music thrummed. The lights
dimmed. The spotlight shone randomly
around the theatre. All the acts were on
the stage, shoulder to shoulder, waiting for
the results. This was it. The moment had
come. I didn't expect to win. Not after the

disaster with the wire. Not after Bottley's betrayal.

But a little part of me wondered if maybe . . . maybe . . . the makeshift, seat-of-the-pants show at the end might have swayed a couple of the judges. I had been good. I had been funny. I'd made the crowd gasp and laugh, and I'd had thunderous applause at the end.

Maybe . . .

'Max Magic!' Willow cried, her voice reverberating throughout the theatre.

My heart sank. I breathed in deeply. But the loss still hurt. The crowd cheered and applauded, but it washed over me. Nothing could save me now. There would be no money, no paparazzi, no limos or helicopters.

Worst of all, though, Mr Mysterio was going to win. And who knew what revenge he was going to take on me for being here in the first place?

'Max put on a brilliant show, as I'm sure you all agree,' Willow said, 'but I'm afraid we had to take away some points because his main trick didn't work. He pulled it back a lot with his impromptu performance at the end, but ultimately we felt that it wasn't enough.'

I felt sick. It was all Bottley's fault. Why had he done this? I felt my chest tingle as the anger rose in me. I forced it down. I couldn't use my powers to take revenge. That's what Michael Lewis would do. That's what Bottley himself would do.

 311

I had to be better than that. I had to control my temper.

'In second place . . .' Willow went on. The spotlights flashed again, and the music thrummed.

I caught Mr Mysterio's eye. He was looking straight at me. I couldn't see through the mask, but I could tell he was smirking. I opened my mind to his.

'I'm going to blast you with a fireball, loser,' he was thinking. 'And that old woman.'

'Bad luck,' he whispered to me.

'It's . . . Mr Mysterio!' Willow cried.

'What?!' he screamed. 'Second?!' He turned to Willow and held up a hand, clearly furious.

Willow took a step back from him, looking surprised by his anger.

'I was beaten by a **dance troupe**?!' he cried.

'Bad luck,' I whispered. I wanted to shout and pump my fists in the air.

Inclusivity were already celebrating. They went leaping and cartwheeling across the stage, whooping and hollering.

'So, our winners tonight are Inclusivity!' Willow yelled, but her voice was drowned out by the roars of the crowd, who were on their feet screaming and cheering.

I was delighted that Mr Mysterio hadn't won, but even better than that was watching the victory of this charming, brilliant group of amazing dancers.

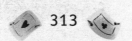

Suddenly, I realised that everything had worked out perfectly. It was destiny, it was chi.

So this is what a balanced universe feels like, I thought.

But then things started happening. Quickly.

Mr Mysterio lunged forward and grabbed hold of Willow Holloughby, who shrieked. Mr Mysterio clamped a hand over her mouth, muffling her. Then before anyone could move, they both disappeared.

Some people in the audience shouted out in shock. But most were watching Inclusivity, who were still leaping about, oblivious to the drama.

This wasn't good. My mind raced

furiously. I hadn't realised that Mr Mysterio might have the power to make other people turn invisible as well as himself. And since no one could see him, no one could stop him. As soon as he left the stage, that would be it. He would be impossible to find, and so would poor Willow!

I had to do something! But what?

I closed my eyes and breathed in, like Mum had shown me in the pyramid. The universe would know what to do, I told myself. And then it came to me.

A genuine showstopper.

I took a deep breath and let the tingle in my chest grow. This time I didn't push it back down. All the anger, all the frustration, all the disappointment – I let it build. I was going to need a lot of power for what I had planned.

I pointed a finger and the stage split open down the middle, revealing a wide chasm, billowing with smoke and heat. Out shot a huge, scaly dragon with vicious teeth, a long, spiny tail and bright red scales.

Everyone screamed. Even I was terrified, and I had created it. Inclusivity were forgotten as everyone stared at the terrifying monster that had appeared from nowhere. Everyone except me of course. I was looking around the theatre.

And there they were. At the back of the stage, as though they were about to

 317

slip out between the rear curtains. Michael Lewis and Willow Holloughby were staring up at the dragon in terror. My hunch had been right. The shock of the vision had interrupted Michael's spell, just as my illusions were interrupted when I lost concentration.

He was visible again.

'Gotcha,' I said.

Using my telekinesis, I knocked Michael's legs out from under him. Willow took the opportunity to flee.

Lucky came charging onto the stage like a furry rocket and took up position in front of me, snarling, his hackles raised. Behind Lucky came Daisy, Stretch and Sophie, who stood on either side of me.

'Team Max!' Sophie yelled.

'Team Max!' the others chorused.

With my attention diverted, the dragon suddenly disappeared. The crowd gasped in wonder. Mr Mysterio spun around to look at me – I think he'd suddenly realised what had happened.

He roared in fury, scrambled to his feet

and ran towards me. I hesitated. Should I blast him? I didn't want to hurt anyone. But I was saved from having to make a decision by Lucky, who charged. Lucky isn't a big dog, but he was moving awfully fast and he knocked Mr Mysterio off balance. The magician tumbled to the stage and slid to a stop, right in front of me.

He scrambled to his feet once more, raised a hand and pointed it right at me, his face red with rage. He was going to blast me with a fireball, I knew it. I braced myself. There was no time to do anything else.

Snick went the handcuffs.

'If there's one thing I can't abide,' PC Peaceful said, 'it's people disturbing the peace.'

Mr Mysterio looked at him in astonishment.

'We were all having a lovely time in the audience,' PC Peaceful said. 'Then you had to go and spoil it by turning Miss Willow invisible. How could you do that to the nation's sweetheart?!'

'You saw that?' I asked.

'I saw the whole thing,' PC Peaceful said. 'I don't know what trickery he used. Mirrors, probably, but Miss Willow clearly didn't want to be made invisible. So you're going to have to come with me and answer some questions, Mr Mysterio.'

'It was him!' Mr Mysterio said, nodding towards me. 'Max Magic. He has a magic chest and can do illusions. He made that

dragon appear. He's a criminal.'

'He's a very talented magician, clearly,' PC Peaceful said. 'Though it's also true he can be a little rowdy at times.'

'He can read minds!' Mr Mysterio babbled. 'He got his powers from a magic chest!' He lifted up his free hand and pointed a finger at me.

'Max! Watch out,' Lucky said. 'Fireball!'

'I suggest you stop,' I said quickly.

Mr Mysterio blinked and dropped his hand.

'And I suggest you take off your mask,' I said.

He did so.

'Well, if it ain't Michael Lewis,' PC Peaceful said. 'That reporter who's always writing about how the police don't do their jobs properly. I think you'd better come with me, son.'

He made to lead Michael away, but I stopped him. 'Wait a moment, Constable,' I said. 'I just need to have a quick word with him.'

PC Peaceful hesitated, then shrugged.

'Where's my candlestick, you plank?' Gran yelled from the crowd.

I leaned close to Michael Lewis and whispered, 'I suggest you forget all about being a magician.'

'OK,' he replied obediently.

'And I suggest you forget all about me, my gran's shop and the chest that's in the basement.'

323

'Yes, I will,' he said flatly.

'And finally,' I said more loudly, 'I suggest that you turn over a new leaf.'

'Yes,' Michael said. 'That would be sensible.'

'Come on,' PC Peaceful said. 'Let's get down the station and you can tell me all about the magic chest.'

'What magic chest?' Michael said, looking confused.

Then he was led away to great cheers from the crowd, who I think mostly still thought this was all part of the performance.

Lucky leaped joyfully into my arms and slobbered wet kisses all over me. My friends gathered around and hugged me.

Stretch was so excited he did a couple of back flips, ending in a somersault. The Inclusivity dancers gave him a rousing cheer. It seemed half the audience was now onstage, despite the efforts of a team of young people with clipboards.

Then Willow Holloughby was there before me, beaming her beautiful smile.

'I hear I have you to thank for saving me from that awful man,' she said.

'It was n-nothing,' I stuttered.

'But how did you create that incredible illusion?' she asked. 'And why didn't you do anything like that during your act?'

'Those are both very good questions,' I said. 'I could tell you, but magicians never reveal their secrets.' I pulled a bunch of

flowers out of my sleeve and handed it to her. She laughed. Then she gave me a hug and a kiss on the cheek – and that was better than winning £10,000, I can tell you.

'Hey,' Sophie said. 'There's Bottley.'

I spun to see my nemesis cowering in the wings, his face like thunder.

'Maybe it's time Bottley was a little wriggling worm,' I said. I held up a finger, intending to make him drop to the floor and squirm around.

Bottley saw me pointing at him, and his expression turned from anger to fear.

But then I saw Gran. She was standing off to one side, watching me carefully. And her words came back to me: 'People can change if you give them a chance. But sometimes you need to show them what's right, and what's wrong.'

'Bottley,' I said walking over to him. 'Why did you do it? Why did you go through all that just to hurt me?'

He glowered at me sullenly, but said nothing.

'Was this to get back at me for the trick with the giant worm?' I asked. 'Were you jealous of me? Did Michael Lewis offer you money for information about the chest?'

'It's none of those things,' Bottley said. 'I told you before, I bully people. Because I like it. There's nothing more to it than that. And you did look very funny wriggling up there on that hook.'

 327

I nodded.

I smiled.

Then I breathed in, feeling the power rising inside me. It was clear what I had to do now. I could have used my power to hurt Bottley, but I knew that an even better revenge was to help him.

'I suggest that you turn over a new leaf as well. I saw a side of you that was good. That was helpful. A side of you that I could be friends with. So I suggest you change – for real this time. Stop being a bully and start helping people.'

'OK,' Bottley said, nodding. 'I will.' And with that he grabbed a broom and started sweeping the stage.

I grinned. Gran was right. People can

328

change. If you give them a little push in the right direction, that is.

Gran came over and gave me a hug. She was beaming from ear to ear.

'Are you OK, Gran?' I asked.

'I've never been better, Max,' she said. 'Don't you worry about me. You were amazing tonight. Absolutely amazing. The whole family thought so.'

Then Vinny, Chris, Susie and Mum had their turn. There were so many people onstage that the people with the clipboards had given up trying to maintain order. The noise was tremendous, with everyone laughing and talking and calling out. Upbeat music played and the dancers were doing their thing.

Finally, Dad appeared through the throng. He grinned, took off my hat and ruffled my hair. 'Well done, son,' he said.

'Thanks for coming,' I said. 'It was good to see you in the crowd. I'd thought maybe you would be too angry to come.'

'Well, I was angry,' he said, 'but then your gran called me and told me to stop being such a fool. To get down here and support my lad. She made some . . . strong arguments. Looks like I was wrong about telling you to pull out. I'm sorry.'

'You don't have to apologise, Dad,' I said. 'I'm sorry I lied to you. I know you only want what's best for me.'

'Just be yourself, Max,' he said. 'That's what's best for you. And if that means you're Max Magic, or Max the Magnificent, or just plain old Max Mullers, then I'll be happy.'

'I'm sorry I didn't win us the £10,000,' I said.

'We don't need £10,000,' he said. 'Not if we have each other.'

I hugged him. He smelled of the market, and bacon, and . . . just Dad.

And it was magic.

Become a magician with Stephen Mulhern

Scan this QR code to learn brand-new magic tricks!

⭐ **Step-by-step instructions**
⭐ **UNBELIEVABLE magic tricks**
⭐ **Tips from Stephen!**

Learn how to perform an unbelievable card trick!

Amaze your friends with this simple magic trick – all you need is a pack of cards and a table . . .

STEPHEN'S TOP TIP!

*Complete steps 1 to 3 **before** you perform the trick!*

1 Find the four aces in the pack of cards and take them out.

2 Place the two black aces **face up** on the table. Place one red ace at the top of the pack and one red ace at the bottom, facing the same way as the rest of the cards in the pack.

 *Hold the pack of cards with the picture side down so no one can see.*

 3 Tell your audience that you will be using the two black aces to find the red aces in the pack.

 4 Deal the cards on to the table, **face down** in a pile, starting with the very top card.

 5 Ask one of your friends to tell you when to stop.

 6 When they say, 'Stop,' place one black ace **face up** on top of the pile of cards on the table.

7 Place the rest of the pack on top of the black ace, **face down**.

 8 Now pick the whole pack up and once again start dealing the cards face down in a pile .

 9 Ask one of your friends to tell you when to stop.

 10 When they say, 'Stop,' place the **second** black ace **face up** on top of the pile.

 11 Place the rest of the pack on top of the pile, **face down**, and pick up the pack again.

STEPHEN'S TOP TIP!

*For the next step, make sure the pack of cards is in your **right** hand.*

12 Fan the entire pack of cards out on the table, starting with the **bottom card on the left** and **moving to the right**, so that all the cards are face down on the table, except the two black aces.

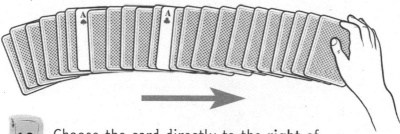

13 Choose the card directly to the **right** of each black ace . . .

14 Turn those two cards over to reveal . . . the two red aces!

Unbelievable!

STEPHEN'S TOP TIP!

Follow along with my video to see this trick step-by-step!

Dress up as Max Magic!

YOU WILL NEED:

1. Normal clothes
2. Playing cards
3. A top hat

Optional:
Lucky the dog!

Don't forget to share your **unbelievable** costume on social media and tag @StephenMulhern & @PiccadillyPress! **DOOSH!**

Can you find Max and all his friends in this magical wordsearch?

```
W  P  S  A  E  D  I  A  R  Y
M  Y  S  T  E  R  I  O  V  M
M  S  R  T  W  G  X  I  D  A
J  A  O  E  R  C  I  W  A  X
L  T  G  P  I  E  S  F  I  P
U  R  A  I  H  M  T  J  S  O
C  B  Q  L  C  I  D  C  Y  W
K  Q  G  Q  E  I  E  O  H  E
Y  C  M  F  F  N  A  G  N  R
I  X  K  J  L  U  T  N  I  S
```

MYSTERIO   **MAX**
TALENT   **SOPHIE**
POWERS   **STRETCH**
MAGICIAN   **DAISY**
DIARY   **LUCKY**

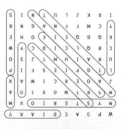

ANSWERS:

MAX

DAISY

SOPHIE

STRETCH

THANK YOU TO . . .

My mum and dad, for inspiring me to follow my dreams. Love you forever.

Jamie, Susie, Chris and Vince, for everything.

Amanda, Millie, Claire, Hannah, Matt and Holly for all your hard work on Max Magic.

Stephen Williams, thank you for all of your help with bringing the magic to life.

Tom, thank you for everything as this exciting journey continues.

Begoña, your art captures Max perfectly. Thank you.

Everyone at Bonnier Books UK, especially – Ruth, Talya, Dom, Nigel, Marina, Rob, Issie, Amber, Jess, Kate and Steph. Ruth, you're an absolute superstar and have understood my vision for Max from the start – I couldn't have done this without you.

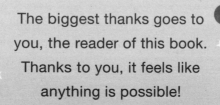

The biggest thanks goes to you, the reader of this book. Thanks to you, it feels like anything is possible!

Tom Easton has published more than forty books for readers of all ages. He has written books about vampires, pirates, teenage girl boxers and teenage boy knitters (not all in the same book). He lives in Surrey with his wife and three children. You can find out more about him at **www.tomeaston.co.uk** or on Twitter @TomEaston

Begoña Fernández Corbalán was born and raised in a small town in Spain. As a child she loved to draw, and after finishing a degree in Fine Arts, she specialised in illustration. She works with watercolour, gouache and pencil as well as illustrating digitally.